UNDER HIS CONTROL

LEONA WHITE

Copyright © 2024 by Leona White

All rights reserved.

No part of this book may be reproduced in any form or by any electronic or mechanical means, including information storage and retrieval systems, without written permission from the author, except for the use of brief quotations in a book review.

❦ Created with Vellum

ALSO BY LEONA WHITE

Mafia Bosses Series

The Irish Arrangement || The Last Vendetta

The Constella Family

Under His Protection || Under His Watch

BLURB

A soldier turned single dad.
    A razor-sharp mafia princess.
    One explosive attraction.

Liam Gray's new reality:
    Surprise toddler. Check.
    Mob job offer. Check.
    Her. Double check.

Eva Constella. 24. Ice queen with a crown of fire.

One scorching night ignites a war:
    Us against the world.
    Desire against duty.
    Hearts against empire.

As enemies circle and bullets fly,
    We face the deadliest threat of all:

Each other.

In this game of love and loyalty,
    There's no safe word.

"Under His Control" detonates with white-hot chemistry and lethal family ties. Strap in for a protective alpha, a fierce mafia princess, and a passion that could topple empires. This ain't your grandma's bedtime story.

1

LIAM

I spent the last several years on planes and flying off to all kinds of locations. Most were dangerous destinations. The missions were for combat or to offer backup for those fighting. My fellow passengers were the other members of my troop.

But no flight had ever given me so much terror and confusion as this one.

"She is just *adorable!*" the gray-haired woman seated next to me exclaimed. Her glasses lifted up on her nose as she used her whole face to smile a full-wattage grin at the person sitting on my lap.

The toddler—*or is she a baby still?*—peered up at me in utter bewilderment.

"How old is she?" the woman asked, making silly smiles at the infant.

She was mine. But I drew a blank and couldn't answer right away. My mind was still lagging on the *you have a child* shock. The paralysis that came with the thought of *you are a dad* was even worse. "Uh, over one."

The woman blinked as the plane lifted for takeoff. "Over one?"

I nodded, glancing back at Olivia Marie Gannon. *My* daughter, courtesy of a one-night stand two years ago. She would now become

Olivia Marie Gray, but I wasn't sure if she or I knew how to make the transition of her being my kid or my being her father.

Taking a closer look at me, raking her curious gaze from my buzz-cut hair that was already growing out too fast to my shirt and jeans, then finally my boots, she twitched her lips. "Ah. You're military, huh?"

"Was."

"Thank you for your service," she replied kindly. "Recently discharged? If I may ask."

"Yes." In hindsight, maybe it was the universe giving me a sign or something. When it was time to sign up for another tour with the alternative offer of a medical discharge for an injury from combat, I considered how my grandfather passed away with one regret—not spending enough time with my grandma when he could. I didn't have anyone but my troop members. I was a bachelor for so long, I doubted I could be anything else.

I hesitated to sign up for more of the military, something in lighter duty with the scars I'd received. When I received word that I'd fathered a baby with Pamela Gannon, a one-night stand who'd passed away, it seemed something else was in store for me. Fatherhood, because I was the dad and no one else could take the baby.

"I won't waste time asking if she's yours," the woman asked, gesturing at Olivia. "She looks so much like you."

"Yeah." I sighed and looked at Olivia again, wondering what in the hell was going on in her little head. What did babies think about? Or was she a toddler? I was so clueless, I couldn't recall the difference.

"But she's new in your life too, huh?"

"Very new," I admitted.

"Aww..." She gazed at Olivia, then me, with hearts in her eyes. "And now she can meet her daddy. I love these welcome-home stories. My son, bless his heart, died several years ago in 'friendly fire'. Mind you, he was only engaged at the time, so he wasn't leaving a little one behind, but I still remember every time he flew home and how we'd make signs and all."

"I'm sorry for your loss."

She dipped her chin. "Thank you. Forgive me for being so chatty. Flights make me nervous. I can just tell you're military. You've got that look. That stance."

That inability to ever shut off the instinct to be alert and assess every moment of your life for dangers and threats? Yeah, she'd recognize it in me, but I didn't care. It was who I was. I was a fighter, a protector, a provider. It looked like I would now need to refine those traits into something that would pass as being a parent, but I'd figure it out one way or another.

Olivia shifted on my lap, not quite wiggling but moving.

Just like I had in the few hours since I picked her up in Utah, where Pamela had lived before passing away unexpectedly in a car accident, I tensed and waited for another cue. Baby—*toddler?*—cues weren't a language that I'd learned yet. I doubted anyone could know how to read a toddler after a mere few hours and be aware of what the hell they wanted or needed.

When she cried in the car ride to the airport, I damn near had a breakdown trying to troubleshoot what she wanted. Googling wasn't fast enough. The uber driver only spoke Russian, but with gestures, he got me to try a bottle of formula that Olivia's daycare owner had told me to use. Thank God I gave her my email. Those lengthy tutorials and typed-out instructions were now the manual I'd swear by.

What is it now? What do you want? What's wrong? If she cried on this plane... Fuck. All the passengers would riot because I had no clue how to help her.

"I think she's tired."

I jerked my face toward the woman next to us. "How? How do you know?"

She smiled softly. "You're *really* new to this, aren't you?"

"Yes. I didn't know Olivia existed until a couple of days ago."

She raised her brows. "Oh, Olivia is such a beautiful name."

I shrugged, watching Olivia as she scrunched her face like she was about to wail. "Her mom named her, then never told me that she existed. She was killed in a drunk driving accident a week ago." I didn't make a habit of talking to strangers, much less about my personal life or that of my daughter's, but I'd never see this woman again. This wasn't a covert mission. Enemies couldn't be listening. I was a civilian now, not in the service. That adjustment was just as hard—if not harder—than suddenly being a dad.

"Oh, honey." The woman placed her hand on my forearm. "That's just terrible. You're really thrust into all of this, huh?"

"Yes." *Fuck.*

Olivia's lips trembled so much that her pacifier fell out. With that indrawn breath, she braced to let out a mighty cry.

Fuck. Fuck. Fuck. "No. No, no, no." I grabbed the pacifier and offered it to her. "Don't cry. Please." I doubted begging would work, but I had to make her hear me.

"Can I help?" the woman asked.

I whipped to face her again. "You can do that?" She said she had a son who was killed in combat. She had been a mother to a baby at one point.

"Sure, sure." She chuckled lightly, holding her hands out. "I'm Jessica. Oh, Olivia, you sleepy little thing."

As I handed my daughter over to the grandmotherly woman, she cooed and smiled, acting all receptive and sweet and nice. All things that weren't *me* or how I knew how to pretend to be.

I cared. Even though this was all so fucking new and shocking, I cared. At first glance, seeing that Olivia was mine, I loved her on the spot. But love and goodwill did not in any way make up for experience or knowhow—of any kind.

"I'm a nurse at a pediatric office too." Jessica winked at me.

I tried to smile to show my genuine gratitude as she held and cuddled Olivia, but I couldn't stop watching and trying to memorize all that she did. The way she held her, how she rubbed her back. All these tricks of the trade that I'd need to figure out on my own.

Unless I ask Jessica if I could just follow her and learn this dark magic of soothing a kid.

All the while, she talked me through steps and suggestions for how to soothe her and hold her better. When Olivia was sleepier, Jessica handed her back over, teaching me how to keep her in my arms—not like she was a bomb about to go off, but as a little human needing security.

Throughout the flight, she lectured and rambled. It was a beginner's course to handling a baby, but I absorbed every single word. I was clueless, and past the surprise that I was a dad, I wondered if I would ever actually get used to this dynamic of being two. Not a bachelor. Not a soldier. A father-and-daughter duo.

"When was she born?" Jessica asked, still smiling at Olivia now sleeping in my arms.

I told her what Olivia's daycare owner told me. That was how little family Pamela had. She'd dropped Olivia off on her way to go to work, and when she didn't come back to pick her up, the daycare owner called the cops and kept her with her until the law enforcement and Children's Services could get involved.

"Oh, okay. So she's thirteen months old."

"I told you that," I said.

"No. You said over a year." Jessica smiled again. "In these years, you go by months."

I furrowed my brow. "For how long?" That seemed kind of strange.

"Well, if you ask my daughter-in-law who never visits me enough, until they're three years old." She giggled at my incredulous expression. "I know. I know. Sounds silly. Usually, until they're two. You stop and shorten it to fifteen or eighteen months. I think most parents generalize from eighteen months to 'almost two' for brevity's sake. Otherwise, you're putting people on the spot to do math." She winked.

For the rest of the flight, she showed me websites, social media groups, and even books that she would recommend for me to read and follow. "Don't go listening to every damn social influencer out there, now." She rolled her eyes. "Most of them don't know what they're talking about and are just pushing a product for affiliation money."

I nodded. That was true of any kind of social media, I assumed, and that was why I seldom used it or went on it.

"Are you flying home, then?" she asked near the end of the flight.

I dreaded saying goodbye to this helpful woman. I didn't often get superstitious or believe in the otherworldly, but she was like a guardian angel just appearing when I needed help, even just to talk and ask questions of without sounding like an idiot.

"Not yet." I wasn't sure where home was or where it could be anymore. I grew up outside New York, raised by my grandparents, but they were both long-gone. I didn't know where I should raise Olivia, but I needed a place to stay and a job to start our future together.

"I'm flying to catch up with an old friend." Tessa West and I had grown up together, sort of. She was younger, but we played together in the apartment building.

"Oh, that's good. Find your village and lean on them. It really does take more than one to raise a child."

I didn't take offense. I knew she wasn't saying that as a dig at me, that I was a single dad. And she was right. Tessa and I had that kind of childhood, growing up in the same building with all kinds of adults and other kids around.

A couple of hours later, after disembarking and getting a ride to the address Tessa gave me, though, I had no clue what to expect from where she'd ended up in life.

Our calls were sporadic since I left the military, but she'd given me some details to wonder about. She recently met her fiancé. She'd moved to his place. And she would love to have me come stay with her for a while and catch up.

Without any other landing strip or directions for where to go and how to adjust to Olivia, I took Tessa up on the invitation. That was how few people I had in my life.

Or not. I glanced at Olivia still sleeping against my chest as I climbed out of the Uber. I would always have Olivia with me now. It hadn't sunk in as a reassuring thought yet, still too new and more like a responsibility to oversee than a companionship to know I wasn't a true loner.

"What the hell?" I muttered, gazing around at this lavish, manicured area. A fucking mansion? Immaculate landscapes, privacy gates, and patrolling security guards?

What in the fuck? Just who the hell was she marrying? Someone rich, clearly, but that made me more guarded.

I glanced around as I walked up the path leading toward the huge house.

"Good evening, sir." A guard at the gate raised his brows at Olivia waking up in my arms.

"I'm..." I huffed. "I'm lost."

The man smiled as his partner stooped down to pick up the pacifier Olivia dropped. He brushed it off and handed it to her. "Where are you headed?"

I blinked and shook my head. "I'm supposed to catch up with my friend, Tessa, but—"

"Right this way, sir," the first guard said. He looked me over. "Liam Gray?"

I gaped at him. "What the fuck?" I whispered. I was in the right place? I didn't know how or why, but I figured, like everything else of late, that I'd roll with the goddamn punches. After finding out I had a kid and that I'd be a civilian now, learning that Tessa was marrying up shouldn't have been too out there. I supposed, in every sense of the phrase, that anything was possible.

The guard led me toward the side, across an enormous patio, then opened the doors to a small gathering inside.

There she was. Tessa looked gorgeous, so happy—and shocked. Her mouth hung open as I entered, reacting just as I figured she might when I revealed what my big surprise was.

"A *baby?*" she exclaimed.

I shrugged and tried to smile when scoping out the room. "Surprise."

A tatted-up man pressed his fingers up under her chin so she'd close her mouth.

"Since when..." Nina, Tessa's old friend, shook her head, walking up.

"Well." An older man strode forward. "Since they've forgotten how to say a simple hello, welcome to our home. I'm Dante Constella." He held out his hand, and I shook it the best I could while holding Olivia, who wanted to squirm.

"Nice to meet ya." I glanced him up and down, wondering who he was.

"A *daughter?*" Tessa asked. "You have a daughter?"

"Yeah."

"But... *how?*"

"I got a letter that I had a kid, and…" I whooshed out a long breath. "And here I am."

"Recently?" Nina asked.

I nodded, raking my hand through my hair as I looked them all over. "Yeah. Very recently. Olivia is a very recent discovery in my life."

Olivia took that moment to pout, then sniffled with pending tears. With everyone dressed up for this engagement party that I was already late for, I felt my eyes go wide, preparing for a wail that I wouldn't know how to stop. Already, the advice Jessica gave me on the plane was forgotten. "Shit. Which cry is this? What's wrong?"

"Oh, darling," a tall, Black woman cooed, rushing from the kitchen where she'd been lingering, away from the guests. "Want a hand with her? I'm the family doctor, Danicia."

"Nice to meet you," I said as I let her take her. "But she's not ill." *I hope? I don't think she's ill? Babies just cry, right?*

She smiled, regardless of Olivia's cries. "Oh, of course not. But you look petrified and clueless."

I nodded, amazed at how a little bounce in her step and sway distracted Olivia.

Do they teach a course on that? Bounce and sway? How does it work? I grimaced, watching how Olivia settled quickly. *God, I have so much to learn.*

The man with Tess chuckled as the family's doctor bounced and swayed with the toddler. "What would you like to drink?" he asked as he held Tess's hand and brought her closer.

"Hi, Liam," Tess greeted, belatedly, as we hugged. She stepped back to the man. "This is Romeo, my fiancé."

I shook his hand, but before I could get a good read on him, Romeo—seemingly quick to notice my discomfort and figuring out that I needed saving—repeated his drink offer.

"Got any decent beer?" I asked, half joking and half sarcastic.

As a member of the kitchen staff nodded and went to fetch my drink, I was again rocked by how posh and extravagant this place was. A family doctor? Staff to wait on them? Holy shit.

"Danicia seems to have Olivia smiling and happy," Tess commented as Danicia and Nina cooed at the girl.

I grunted a laugh. "Better than I can."

"Rough going?" Romeo guessed.

"Yeah. Very rough," I admitted. "Sorry I'm underdressed for whatever you've got planned tonight."

Tess patted my arm. "You're going to have to fill me in on a *lot* more details. But later. Right now, I'm excited for you to meet the family before we join the party."

Meet the family? Funny, I just met more of mine—family I didn't know I had.

2

EVA

"Maybe *I* should get a job." I mumbled the bitter comment for my ears only, but I wasn't alone at the bar like I thought I was.

"You?" Franco asked, laughing once. The family's highest-ranking capo joined me at the bar as I helped myself to a drink. He leaned over to get a water out of the fridge, opting to stay sober instead of giving himself a night off from all the security matters of our lives.

Security was always a priority, especially with the Constellas waging war—or preparing to—against the Giovanni Family and that damn Devil's Brothers MC.

Tonight was supposed to be a chance for all of us to relax and celebrate, to be happy for Tessa and Romeo while Dante and Nina hosted their engagement party here at the mansion.

"Why the hell would you be job hunting?" Franco asked, as if I couldn't have said anything crazier.

"Because it would give me something to do." I arched my brows at him. "Why else does anyone get a job?"

He smirked. "Well, for those who aren't born into the lap of wealth like you, people need money."

"I realize that," I replied dryly. "Of course I know that." I never asked to be born into this family. I never asked for my parents to be killed when I was a young child, to be raised by Dante Constella and taught propriety and entitlement. I didn't blame my uncle for spoiling me, but we all knew I was revered and respected as something like royalty.

Mafia princess. The term was starting to grate on my nerves more and more now. When I was younger, Romeo could get away with teasing me about the moniker that our peers gave me, that I was the icy Mafia princess, haughty and superior.

No one other than my uncle and cousin—maybe Franco here, too—knew that it was all a façade I hid behind, a mask to protect who I really was deep down.

The only problem was that I no longer could be certain I knew who I was anymore.

I was still Dante's niece, but with Nina engaged to him and expecting his baby, I wasn't as important to nag after him and make sure he wasn't working too hard.

I was still Romeo's cousin, but with Tessa celebrating her engagement to him tonight, I wouldn't be as involved in his life anymore, either.

"Then why would you need a job?" Franco asked. "For fuck's sake. Don't I have enough issues to deal with? If you get it in your head to go find a career, that'll be a whole extra crew that I'll need to staff to follow you and vet out the security at wherever you go."

"I'm not saying I need a job." He was right. I didn't need money. "But it wouldn't be so bad to have a…"

He put his water bottle to his mouth, waiting for my reply as he drank.

"A purpose."

As he lowered the bottle, he pointed at me with a finger not wrapped around the plastic. "Aha. I knew it."

"Knew what?" Nothing pissed me off more than someone presuming to *know* me. Franco did. He'd been in a high position for Dante and Romeo for so long that he was well aware of everything about my life, and that of my uncle and cousin. I'd spent so long and practiced for years to hide myself that I became instantly aggravated when anyone supposed they saw the real me.

"It's getting to you, too," He nodded, looking off to the side with less of a smug expression. "Them getting married."

"No one's getting married *yet*," I argued. He made it sound like we were attending back-to-back weddings.

He shrugged. "With them getting engaged. Nina and Dante expecting. Now, Romeo and Tessa." He shook his head. "They both met their other half and boom, all of a sudden, they're all in domestic bliss."

I pressed my lips together and ran my tongue along the inner seam, keeping my words locked in. He'd hit the nail on the head there. Every word was true. While I should've felt some consolation in the fact that Franco could commiserate with what I was saying, it didn't make me feel any better.

"I've wondered why you've been extra aloof lately." He leaned his forearms on the bar like I'd stooped to do. The room was empty, but a member of the house's wait staff who was hired for the engagement party slipped in to get a beer bottle from this private room.

"I'm not extra aloof," I protested.

"Oh, cut the shit, Eva." Franco was one of the few men who could talk to me like this and get away with it. Dante and Romeo were the only others.

"It's just you and me talking in here," he said. "If it helps, I've been feeling the same."

I furrowed my brow, wishing that weren't true. If Franco was experiencing the same dejection that I was dealing with, I'd hate for him to suffer. "Like what?"

He shrugged and let out a gusty sigh. "Like feeling sorry for myself that I don't have anyone."

I nodded when he glanced at me, confirming what he said. "Yeah. I hate that I am, but I've been feeling jealous of Dante and Romeo." I held up my hand and cleared my throat. "Don't get me wrong. I like Nina and Tessa."

He grunted. "Not at first."

"But once I got to know them, I did." I wouldn't apologize for

UNDER HIS CONTROL

being overprotective of them. When Nina showed up in the house, she seemed to be a gold-digger out to use my uncle Dante as a sugar daddy. Only once I saw how they tried to hide their attraction for each other did I realize they had a true connection.

"But I wish I had someone like that. Someone for myself."

He set his water down and hung his head lower. "And now you're thinking, in typical independent, Mafia-princess fashion, that maybe you don't need someone to spend your life with but something to spend your life on?"

Dammit. He was too damn good at reading me. "Maybe."

He stood, stretching his back. "That's like what Dante did before. And you can't deny that he's happier now. He was married to work. Then he met Nina, and now look at him."

Again, he was correct. My uncle had always been busy as the boss of the family. Romeo, too, and he was so damn serious. Both men were infinitely happier now since meeting their partners.

That just makes me feel worse. Thanks.

"You don't know what it's like, though. You've got your job, your purpose and mission." I frowned at him. "And I'm not even allowed to have a job because of the security issues it'd create."

He rolled his eyes. "Oh, don't give me that shit. I was teasing. Mostly. You and I both know you can and will do whatever the hell you want. You won't get far in convincing anyone that you're stuck or confined with the power and money you have in this family."

"But I am stuck and confined in finding someone because of the power and money I have in this family." I turned toward him and crossed my arms, defensive like usual. "Try to tell me that's not true."

"Fine. It is." He stepped away from the bar and put his arm around my shoulders, steering me out of the room to join the rest of them waiting to go into the ballroom for the party. "Most of the assholes in our world wouldn't be good enough for you. And every one of them would want to use you for leverage."

I nodded as I walked out with him.

"I don't know that you can claim I'm any better off for having my job and mission." He instantly scanned the room where everyone else was waiting, always on edge and quick to check for threats.

"Because it wears on you? Being *on* all the time?"

"No. That's just who I am. I mean knowing how different it can be to have someone to spend your life with. I think about her."

Chloe? Still? I didn't have to ask who he was referencing.

"It's been..."

"Ten years," he replied without missing a beat. "And I wonder every fucking day why she left."

I patted his hand that draped over my shoulder. I noticed that Franco didn't talk about it much with Dante and Romeo, but he was vulnerable with me, telling me that he missed his former flame.

That sounded like an even worse fate. To have love and lose it, versus never having it at all?

Again, maybe I should just get a job. It would be helpful to distract myself, to be preoccupied and not dwell on being single for seemingly forever.

But what the hell would I do?

Any job that I got would be a pity offering, someone giving me a position just because I was a Constella and Dante wielded so much power.

It's all a lost cause. I'm a lost cause.

I let that sentiment sink in as I mingled and made my way through the engagement party. Like with all other events hosted at the mansion, the ballroom was decorated to show off the elegance of the architecture without being too much. All the guests drank and chatted. Romeo and Tessa smiled at everyone who'd come to wish them well, and more than a few also spoke with Nina who was just about to clear the end of her second trimester.

Happy, peppy couples, all around. And then there's me.

Bitterness seeped through me, worsening my frustration that I didn't know how to climb out of this funky gloom and despair.

"What, no ice sculpture fountains full of champagne?"

I turned, pausing in walking away from a table near one of the bars where the servers loaded up their trays with flutes of the drink. The man who'd spoken likely had done so to talk to himself. Even if it wasn't a gruff line of snark, scoffing that complaint and mocking the party, he'd said it low and quiet, as though he didn't count on anyone overhearing.

As though he didn't anticipate that I'd be passing by and stop at the complaint about anything my family offered.

"The beverages aren't to your liking?" I sassed as I spun to face him.

While his white button-down was simple, the rest of him wasn't. His jeans—*jeans!*—were so worn and weathered they had to be the only comfortable garment anyone had on in this ballroom. His boots were covered with a faint trace of dust, and his hair, while slightly too long, wasn't styled at all.

Who invited this cowboy here?

I'd never seen him before, but now that I faced him directly, getting the full burn of his glare, I wondered if he'd entered the back of the house earlier and we'd just happened to pass by each other in that room, when I was talking to Franco.

This engagement party wasn't a full-on black tie affair, but a little care for decorum was required. And this guy either didn't care or didn't know. Strangers wouldn't be permitted. Franco's security forces would weed out any trespassers. Which begged the question of who the hell invited this underdressed, rugged, sexy-as-hell—

Hold up.

I shook my head, annoyed with how quickly my mind derailed under his smirking glare. I was *not* going to notice how attractive this rebel was. Not now. No how.

"My beverage is fine." He proved it in tipping back the beer bottle. "But the uppity pretension in this place is not."

Uppity? "Then maybe you're in the wrong place?" I set my hand on my hip. I'd be damned if some low-class idiot said my family was uppity. For many generations, the Constellas had sacrificed so much to promise our future would be prosperous and thriving. This nobody didn't know what he was talking about. We weren't pretentious. Or uppity. Or—

Oh, my God. Why do I even care what this guy thinks?

"Let me guess," he deadpanned. "Wrong place at the wrong time?"

I crossed my arms, immediately bristling at his challenging, droll tone. Something about him set me on edge and made me want to argue—more than I already usually did. This man, who clearly couldn't belong, just rubbed me the wrong way.

"Something tells me there will never be a right time for *you* to belong here."

He rolled his eyes and set his empty beer bottle down on the table. "Great. *Another* stuck-up bitch who can look at me like I'm something the cat dragged in. This party is a blast."

Stuck-up bitch? His first mistake was in assuming I was like any other woman here. And his second was his guess that his words would make an impact on my night. I knew my worth, and he never would. I was an intelligent, confident woman, and no plebeian like him would wound me with his inferior opinions. But it sure as hell didn't mean I had to put up with it.

"Get out."

He huffed. "Yeah, right."

"I don't know how you get in here, but you clearly weren't invited if you intend to attack the Constella name."

"Oh." Slight surprise lit up his striking blue eyes. I hated that they were so gorgeous, so alluring and drawing me in. Especially when his tone was so mocking. "You're one of the Constellas?"

Who was this man? How could he not know where he was or who he was speaking to? As I furrowed my brow, trying to puzzle out how a stranger could get this far into the mansion, Romeo approached.

"There you are," he said, holding his arm out to place it around my side.

"Another 'family' member?" the stranger guessed, placing a sarcastic emphasis on that one word.

"Yes." Romeo nodded. "Liam, meet my cousin, Eva."

He looked up me and down, taking a good, long look of me in my short dress. "Hmm." He didn't extend his hand to shake mine, a deliberate insult, no doubt, with how we'd already exchanged words.

Romeo frowned a bit but didn't lose his stride. "Eva, this is Liam Gray. Tess's friend."

I'd be damned if I offered my hand to him. As far as introductions went, this one rated sub-zero in temperature and a high exponent of hostility. Since I had his full attention, I let him feel the pressure of my stare as I took him in. Every lean, muscled, and rugged inch of his tall frame.

Handsome asshole.

I held my head up higher, letting him see how far I was out of his league.

"Eva," Romeo prompted, squeezing my shoulder. "Help me welcome Liam," he said through clenched teeth.

"Welcome him?" I asked.

This was just a party. He'd be going as soon as it was over.

One glance up at my cousin suggested otherwise. The tense expression he gave me also implied that he disliked how rudely I was behaving.

"Tess has offered for him to stay with us for a while. To visit."

Fuck it all. So much for thinking he wouldn't be here for more than one night as a guest who didn't belong.

Romeo squeezed his fingers on my shoulder a little more.

Keeping my lips tight together, I refrained from scowling or giving any sign that the indifference I was showing was false. I looked Liam dead in his gorgeous blue eyes that were dancing with mischief and held out my hand.

"Nice to meet you," I lied. *Judgmental asshole.*

"Likewise," he said, likely lying through his teeth with a smirk on his lips. He took my hand, stunning me with the zing of awareness at his calloused hand touching me with what should've been a simple gesture of greeting.

It felt like anything but. It felt like… a dare. A challenge. And I wasn't sure whether I'd want to back down from whoever the hell Liam Gray was.

3

LIAM

Thanks. *Thanks for reminding me that I don't belong here, Eva.*
I listened to Romeo as he spoke about introducing me to another cousin, a distant one named Franco, but I couldn't take my focus off the silent, brooding Eva standing next to him.

I knew from the second I walked into this extravagant ballroom that I didn't belong. Once I began to meet some of the "family" gathered here to celebrate Romeo and Tessa's engagement, I realized it wasn't only a group of Constella relatives, but the fucking Mafia.

What in the hell are you thinking, Tessa?

As if life hadn't thrown me enough curveballs lately. First, leaving the military, something that I never thought I'd willingly do. Second, the news that I was a father. Third, that my childhood friend was marrying into the goddamn Mafia.

I'd fallen into a rabbit hole and ended up in a bizarre world. None of this seemed right. Nothing sounded like it made sense anymore. I could roll with the punches. I wasn't impervious to changes. But this was too much.

An awkward silence filled in among the three of us. I didn't know what to say. Small talk wasn't my thing on the best of days, and I had no clue who these people were.

Romeo seemed impatient to get back to Tessa, making me wonder if he was controlling her.

Eva was trying her damnedest not to check me out even though her icy once-over promised that she found me lacking.

And I had no clue how long I should leave Olivia with Danicia—who'd asked for my phone to text me updates of Olivia playing with toys in a living room somewhere in this place.

Eva caved to the pressure first, clearing her throat. "I see Dante looking for us." She tugged on Romeo's sleeve, and with a polite but insincere smile that she tossed my way as an excuse to leave, she led her cousin away.

"Yeah. Whatever. Good riddance." I watched them go toward the Mafia Boss. Once they crossed the ballroom, I hurried to cut through the crowd and find my friend. Passing all the rich and fancy guests, I ignored the overwhelming sensation of being in the dark.

Nothing about this was adding up. The last I'd heard from Tessa, she was still waitressing at a steakhouse. Still worried about her parents wanting her to marry some lawyer. Still poor and doing the best she could to eke out a life.

Not laughing and smiling in a designer gown, joking and mingling without a care in the world at this mansion guarded by Mafia men.

And I was determined to get some answers about how and why this change had happened.

"Hey, Tessa," I said.

"Liam!" She beamed, her face lighting up with joy. The shorter bob was a new cut from what I remembered when we were younger, before I was deployed, but it suited her. Never minding my confusion and suspicion, she looked good. And content.

"Are you having fun? I know you're not a big partier. Or maybe that's changed over the years, but I hope you're enjoying yourself so far."

I nodded, tipping my head for her to follow me to the side. "Uh, that's not the only thing that's changed."

She laughed, so bright and cheerful as she stepped toward the side with me. "Uh, yeah! I'm still shocked that you have a baby!"

"I think she qualifies as a toddler. Maybe?" I ran my hand through my hair, checking whether any Mafia goons were lurking close enough to hear us.

"Just the fact that you have a child, Liam. That's huge news."

I stepped closer so we could whisper. "So is the fact that you're marrying into the fucking Mafia."

Her smile dimmed and she sighed heavily. "Okay, so, it's not what you think."

"Not what I think?" I scoffed. "The Constellas are a fucking Mafia Family."

"Yes, but—"

"No *but*, Tessa. For fuck's sake. Are you insane? What are you thinking?"

She narrowed her eyes, getting testy with my outburst that I struggled to keep quiet.

"Look, I know life's been hard."

"When wasn't it?" she retorted.

Always. We'd grown up without much, not in poverty but lower middle-class. "That's not any excuse." I stepped closer and set my hands on my hips. "Is that fucker forcing you to marry him? Is he controlling you?"

She rolled her eyes. "Cut it out. Seriously. We stay in touch while you're overseas for how many years, and now the second you're back you're going to act like some protective big brother?"

Back when we were younger, I had acted like that. I did step up to look out for her like a big brother might have, but when I was away and serving in the military… I hadn't been here for her.

"Just make it make sense." I heaved out a long breath, wondering if I could suspend my disbelief to hear her out with whatever excuse she'd give me.

"Why would you think he's controlling me?" She crossed her arms.

"I've been watching him."

She rolled her eyes, still miffed. "That doesn't shock me. You've probably been looking for an enemy all night, just the same as you're clocking all the exits."

I raised my brows, silently showing her that she was right and we both knew it. "I've been watching the way he acts when he's around you and when he steps away. He's obsessive about checking where you are."

"Because I was almost killed or captured by his enemies. Twice."

I groaned, turning away. "And you're still interested in marrying him? Signing up for a life of constant danger?"

"Oh!" She grabbed my arm and turned me back. "That's rich, hearing that from *you*. A life of constant danger? What, like someone in combat?"

"We're talking about you, not me." I shook my head and gently held her upper arms. I ducked so I was more at her eye level, prompting her to focus on me. "Tessa. The Mafia? Come on. This is insane."

"No, it's not." She stood up straighter. "Romeo habitually checks on where I am because he's protective of me, Liam. Not controlling. Ever since he saved me the night..." She looked down and paused to take in a deep breath.

Watching her struggle to find words worried me.

"The night three men chased me down and raped me, he's been *very* protective and concerned about my safety and happiness."

"What?"

She winced and pushed my hands off. I didn't mean to squeeze hard, but I had.

"Sorry." I opened and closed my mouth, furious and shocked. "Did you say...?"

"Yes." She nodded, but I saw the lingering effects of trauma in her gaze. It had to be hard to even say that, let alone think it, but she wasn't cowering from the truth of it. "They chased me and... and violated me. He saved me that night, and every minute since then, he's made it his goal to ensure my safety and happiness."

"Holy fuck." I turned again, rubbing my hand over my face. Anger pummeled through me at the fact that she'd ever suffered that fate, but deep regret swiftly followed.

Some older brother figure I was. While I was gone, that happened. I hadn't been here to help her with that trauma.

"Romeo is my hero," she said, tugging my hand to make me face her again, imploring me to listen.

Hero? A Mafia boss as a hero? Disbelief struck me hard.

It sounded like an oxymoron that I couldn't get behind. She wouldn't convince me that easily. Maybe Romeo was conveniently there when she needed someone to intervene, a case of being there to help her when something bad happened. His doing one good deed wouldn't make him an instant hero, a good guy just because he did one good thing.

I furrowed my brow, looking around at this place we couldn't fit in. We weren't rich. We weren't at ease on this side of the socioeconomic spectrum. I had some money from being in the military, but it was no wealth to allude to schmoozing with these people.

"Liam, you've got to understand," Tessa argued.

"Understand what?" I snapped. "These people are in the *Mafia*, Tessa. You're associating yourself and your future with syndicated crime bosses."

The Constellas were players in the kind of shit that ruined society. I'd lived through fighting it to know it. Money made the world go round, and often, the leaders who dealt it out were terrorist groups like the ones I fought, or crime lords like the man she claimed to be a hero.

"We will discuss this later," she said. She pursed her lips and looked away, seeming disappointed that I could be so upset and worried for her.

This wasn't a case of disapproving of whom she wanted to marry. It was a matter of not wanting her to be hurt and targeted as a Mafia wife. Romeo's being in the Mafia was a big red flag that I couldn't believe she'd ignore.

She wasn't in the mood to hear me out, though. She wasn't interested in asking me about how I'd come to find out I had a daughter, either. Walking off to join Romeo, she didn't seem excited about talking to me at all.

I growled under my breath as I walked back toward one of the bars. I wouldn't fit in here, but that wouldn't stop me from drinking their booze and numbing some of these shocks that kept coming my way.

Ordering a shot didn't take me long, and drinking it lasted even less.

"Another?" the bartender asked, one brow raised.

I had a high tolerance, but I was doing this to forget for a moment. That I was a father responsible for a toddler. That I had no clue where my life would go. That my friend was intent on marrying into the Mafia.

Before I could reply, my phone chimed with another update from Danicia of Olivia sleeping in a crib.

Danicia: *Nothing wrong with lil Olivia trying out one of the cribs for Nina's baby. :)*

Danicia: *Enjoy the party. She's good for a long while in your guest room with me.*

I nodded. Hell, I probably wouldn't have another chance to drink for a while. Then I shook my head. "A double."

He didn't judge. With a curt nod, he got my drink.

"Looks like the beverages are still to your liking."

I glared at the wall at Eva's taunting voice.

She sidled up to me at the bar, disdain still evident in her eyes and disapproval clear in her frown.

"Fuck." I shook my head. I didn't know why she'd singled me out. Of all the men and women in this big-ass ballroom, she had to target me, to make *my* life more miserable than it already had the potential for. "Not you again."

"Don't make yourself comfortable." She kept looking forward, giving me her profile to scowl at. It wasn't a hardship to gaze at her from this angle. Eva had the classic sort of beauty that would be gorgeous no matter which way I stared at her.

I didn't listen. I did make myself comfortable, taking in every detail. Those regal high cheekbones, the smooth sun-kissed skin, and the cascading wave of her glossy brown locks as they tumbled over her shoulder. I dragged my stare lower, appreciating the toned definition of her arm and wondering how long it would take for her flesh to break out in goosebumps from my caress there. If I were to tug that thin strap off and lower her dress...

I exhaled all the pent-up frustration I didn't want to hold in any longer. She was frigid, an icy woman who made it no secret that I couldn't affiliate with her, but fuck, was she sexy. The attraction between us had flared up as instantly as our annoyance with each other had. Potent and quick to flame.

I wanted her on a visceral, physical level, but now wasn't the time. And she wasn't the woman to lose myself in.

"You belong less than he does." She tipped her chin at the bartender.

Less than the hired help. That was fucking precious.

I stood, buoyed with this infuriating lust for her. She was hot. She was tempting. But way, way too irritating for me to want to spend another moment near her.

"Shut up," I told her, "and stay out of my fucking way."

I knew which battles to fight, and she wouldn't be one. Not if she was a member of the goddamn Mafia I wasn't sure Tessa should marry into. I tried my best not to start a scene with Tessa when I asked her about this family she was interested in joining. And I would try my best not to start a scene with Eva here. Instead, I turned and walked away with the last drink that I'd allow myself for the night.

"You can't talk to me like that," she said, seething as she hurried after me.

I sipped my drink, not giving her the satisfaction of a reply as I headed toward the door that I hoped would lead out of this ritzy, glamorous ballroom that I didn't want to be in.

"I'll talk to you however I want." I glared at her grabbing hold of my sleeve. "And if you don't leave me alone, I'll make you regret it."

She narrowed her eyes. The dark brown in them swirled and glittered with desire, and I resisted the allure of turning her on. She wanted me, just the same as I lusted for her.

"Is that a threat?" She just didn't know when to stop pushing.

I clenched my teeth, fighting the urge to snap and show her how close I was to losing control.

I was mad. Confused. Rootless and angry. From so many fronts. And faced with this teasing need to see if her bite was a bad as her bark, I bordered on wanting to strangle her or fuck her.

"It can be," I warned, realizing that she was enjoying this, too.

4

EVA

No one threatened *me*. Not if they wanted to live.

Yet, Liam just had. He told me to leave him alone, and it was the last thing I wanted to do. He intrigued me. He annoyed me. There was something about him that I couldn't ignore.

"Don't you dare." Glaring up at him, I hated that I had to crane my neck to face him properly. To maintain direct eye contact—which I always did, with everyone so I would not leave room for anyone assuming I was weak or intimidated—I had to almost dip back as we stood so close together. Inches parted us, and the longer I held on to his sleeve, the more this gnawing desire pushed me to grab hold even more.

I wanted to wrap my fingers around his bulging biceps, knowing they wouldn't close over the girth. I needed to push against his chest and find out why his shirt strained over his muscled physique, if he really was that lean. I yearned to push and push, to test him and see how soon he'd snap and act on this tension that set up between us as instantaneously as our mutual loathing had.

His nostrils flared as he glowered down at me. The piercing blue of his eyes sparkled darker. And with the hard press of his lips, so tight together in his scowl, I felt tempted and encouraged to prod at him just that little more, to poke and push his buttons and see him really react.

He stepped closer, into my personal space. "What shouldn't I dare?"

Having him nearly flush to me short-circuited my logic. I couldn't think, I couldn't comprehend a witty comeback. Men didn't have power over me. They didn't intimidate me.

But *he* did. Within each other's space, we were caught in a firestorm of chemistry that ticked closer and closer to combustion.

"Don't you dare tell me what to do," I replied, hating that it wasn't the strongest string of words that I was capable of. *I already said that, didn't I?*

"Listen to me, Eva." He took a chance to step one more foot toward me. The toes of his boots bumped my shoes. His scent hit me, something clean and spicy. His body heat radiated to me, enticing me to curl toward him. As I dragged my gaze up from his chest to find those blazing blue eyes, I licked my lips and wondered if I could still taste his drink on his.

"I've had a shitty few days. Tonight has been nothing but a surprise, and not all of it is favorable."

I steadied my breath, unwilling to show him how much his gravelly, gritty growl turned me on even more. I had no business wanting someone like him. Rough and tumble, rugged, and dressed down, a simple but strong man unlike the glossy, proper Mafia soldiers and men supposedly worthy of someone with my status.

"The last thing I want to do is put up with an icy pain in the ass like you. Mafia diva or not."

Anger charged through me, twisting with the threads of desire he stoked in me.

"If you don't leave me alone and find someone else to pick on…"

Then what? Then what! I had to know. I wanted to learn what he'd try to do. If it included giving in to this sexual tension that I had no way to explain, then I wanted to hear it.

He lowered his head. His breath whipped so hotly over my ear, tickling me and turning me on at the same time. "Then the next time you push me, I'll fuck you so hard that I'll ruin you for any other man in this world."

I shivered and closed my eyes at the vision he painted. His big hands on me. His mouth tasting me. Fingers exploring and teasing. His dick sliding into me.

Oh, God. Please. I need it.

I shouldn't want him, but I did. Inexplicably, I yearned for him to deliver on that filthy threat.

As he stepped back, I opened my eyes and glared at him. "You wouldn't." It was a weak argument, one I doubted. But I couldn't let him have the last word. I didn't know who the hell he was. He was a stranger, not from my world. Regardless, I would never let a man have the last word.

He didn't speak, staring back at me with such an intensity, I wanted to lunge at him and test his theory.

Then he turned, giving me his back and striding through the crowd. I stood there, rooted in place, stunned.

My heart hammered so fast, as though I'd run a marathon. My lungs strained to pull in air, too shallow to fuel the adrenaline rush of being challenged, rejected, and scolded away. The realization that he'd walked away was too much to bear.

That was it. His dismissal. His resistance was what damned us. Because in doing so, in walking away from me and this electric draw and what pulled us together, he'd declared himself off limits. Forbidden. He already *was* forbidden. I had no business lusting after a nobody like him. Wanting him was a form of rebelling—against my life, against this need for a distraction.

I didn't care how weak it would make me, but I had to chase him down.

This was not the end of it. It couldn't be.

No man *ever* told me off and ordered me to back off. And I'd be damned if he considered himself the first one to do it.

Cutting through the crowd, I sought him out. He was so tall, it wouldn't be difficult to find him, but he was stealthy and fast. With all the guests clogging up the room, I only just caught sight of him slipping out the doorway and into the hall.

I'll be damned if you tell me how it is.

I rushed after him, furious and so turned on that those forces seemed the same.

In the hallway, more people blocked me, but I wove around them all. Once the path was clear, I picked up my pace and jogged after him.

"You—"

My remark was cut short. He whirled, catching me around the waist before he turned us. With such a quick, sudden movement, he surprised me, almost as if he'd been counting on me or hoping that I'd seek him out.

Whatever I could've said no longer mattered. His hard, hot mouth crushed against mine. At the first forbidden touch, I moaned at the rush of excitement, of red-hot desire. With just that one kiss, pinning me to the wall of the closet he'd pulled me into, he enflamed me from the inside out.

"I told you," he growled, panting as he broke the kiss.

One kick back at the door slammed it shut. An exit light glowed overhead, casting shadows over his rugged, tense face as he seethed at me.

"I told you what I'd do."

"You don't call the shots," I argued as I grabbed his head and pulled him back for a hard kiss. He grunted into my mouth, parting my lips to slide his tongue in. He fought for dominance, exploring my mouth and forcing me to accommodate him, and damn it, but I gave in. I anted up to his silent demands by kissing back just as hard, and I held on tight, desperate for more and more of this wicked heat and need he requested.

"The fuck I don't," he argued as he roughly wedged his leg between mine, making me spread mine. "You had to push. You wouldn't stop. And now you're getting to get it, you fucking brat."

I groaned at his angry words. It was twisted to be turned on by his gruffness, but I was dripping wet, aroused and needy for his touch. As he shoved up my dress and yanked at my panties, I fumbled for his pants.

"You hear me?" He swatted my hands away, taking over to unzip. "I'm going to fuck the sass out of you. You want a lesson? You want to know what happens when you piss off the wrong man, you fucking slut?"

I closed my fingers around his long, hard length. "Oh, really?" I taunted back. No man spoke to me like this. No one told *me* how it was. And no one ever belittled me and called me a slut. Hearing that degradation from him, though, was a hell of a turn-on. I didn't have any kinks. Until him. Until now.

"You're calling me a slut?" I challenged as I stroked him.

He sucked and kissed, bit and licked all down my neck as he ripped my panties down. My fingers were slick with his precum as I pumped his erection, making sure to feel every rigid inch of his thickness. This was the fastest I'd ever fallen into sex, but it was still taking too damn long. I was rabid for him, but this dirty talk didn't put me out of the mood.

"Yeah. A mouthy, smartass slut." He grunted and thrust into my hand, humping me as I clumsily stepped out of my panties. If he wasn't pinning me to the wall, I would've fallen with how shaky my legs were.

"I'll show you what happens when you don't listen," he growled as he hoisted me against him.

I gasped at the first hard bump of his dick at my entrance. Slippery and throbbing with my juices, he almost speared right into me. I wished he would. I needed him to.

Please. I clung to him, hoping he'd feel how badly I couldn't let him go. I wrapped my arms around his neck at the same time I sealed my lips to his.

This was wrong. He had no right to talk to me like that. He had even less right to secret me into a closet and threaten to fuck me, to ruin me for any other man.

But I wanted it. So, so bad.

"I told you to leave me alone," he said, imprinting that sexy, husky tone in my mind as he rubbed his dick back and forth over my wet entrance. "I told you to fuck off. But now, I'm going to fuck you." He finished his claim by notching his cockhead into me. Even just that tip stretched me. It burned in the best way. I relished the hint of a fullness that would push me to come so fast.

"You hear me, slut? I'll fuck this attitude out of you." He drove in, shoving me up against the wall in one long, swift thrust.

"Fuck! Liam!" I gasped, arching without any room to move, sandwiched between his hard body and the wall. Impaled on his huge dick. Braced between his hands on my ass cheeks, his fingers digging in tight. "Fuck!" I struggled to catch my breath at the brutal, instant force of his cock so deep inside me. All the way. It was too much and not enough in the same stroke of intensity.

"That's right, Eva." He kissed along my jaw, nipping at my sensitive flesh already suffering from the whisker burns of his stubble. "Cry my name. I don't give a shit who hears. You scream me name and let the world know that I'm fucking your tight cunt." He pulled out and slammed in all the way again. "I'll pound this attitude right out of you."

"Oh, fuck." I let my head roll back on the wall. So overwhelmed with the stretch of his girth, I wasn't sure I could handle it. If I could handle him. His rough talk was half the thrill.

"You want me to fuck you, little slut?" He groaned as he rocked back and forth, driving me up against the wall. "You want my dick to fill your pussy?"

"Oh, my God." I slumped back to the unforgiving surface with each of his hard pushes into me. Over and over. He drove into me like a beast. Not stopping once, he thrust into me and slid his hardness over the tender flesh of my pussy until I was on the verge of coming.

"Tell me, Eva. You like being a bratty little slut? Begging for my dick?"

I whined, so lost to the concept of words. All I wanted was that orgasm. It was so close, so teasingly close. Never before had a man fucked me like this, hard, without any preamble other than a threat to ruin me. Right now, bouncing on his dick in a closet, I wanted it. I needed him to ruin me, to satisfy me in such a way I hadn't known I could enjoy.

"Tell me. You want my dick?" he ordered.

"Yes!" I cried out before he kissed me hard. "Yes!"

"Then come, you stuck-up brat. Milk me. Come wrapped around me."

I groaned, so close to shattering that I strained not to lose the momentum of pleasure. It was so fast, so torrid and forbidden, that I couldn't keep up with the intensity of the sensations pummeling me.

"Come, Eva. Come on my dick." He kissed me harder, giving me yet another chance to taste the heat of his flavor and the hint of the liquor he'd drunk. "Squeeze me. Obey me, you fucking bratty slut."

"Liam," I whined, arching my back to get the last bit of friction that would send me over. "Please!"

"Come, Eva. Now. Then every time you think about another man fucking your pussy, you can know that it'll never be as good as this."

He gripped my hair and held me in place for his rough kisses. With my head held steady, my upper body followed suit. Clutching my ass with his other hand, he trapped me in place for him to smack his hips to mine, ensuring his dick pierced into me perfectly.

My thighs trembled at the first waves of my orgasm. It hit me so hard, without pause, that I feared I couldn't hold on, that I couldn't survive the intensity of the bliss exploding.

He didn't drop me as the euphoria burned through my veins. But he melted me, incinerated me inside and out as he pumped into me a few more times then followed me with his release.

I struggled to breathe, contorting my face into a wince as I clung to him and tried to stay afloat. I was dizzy and soaring with the onslaught of sensations that bombarded me with the relief he spurred.

"Fuck," he grunted as he burrowed his face against my neck. He staggered in his step but didn't drop me. "Fuck, Eva. *Fuck*."

I cinched my arms tighter around his neck as I tried to come down from the high of my orgasm, doubting that I'd ever, *ever* be able to face him again. I couldn't. Not if we ended our arguments like *this*.

If he hadn't ruined me for any other man, he sure as hell wrecked me for the rest of the night.

As soon as I could stand, I pushed away from him and ran out the door, afraid of facing his cocky face after proving he was right.

He'd done something to me. He'd made an impression. He'd shown me how damn good it felt to surrender, if only for a quick, hot moment.

With his hot cum leaking out my pussy, I ran out of there to figure out how to get over the lapse of judgment that felt way too good.

5

LIAM

Olivia's baby babbles woke me. Her sounds had been my alarm clock for less than a week. Before her, I was wired to get up per military time. Since coming home with no direction but to somehow force myself to be a father, my sense of time was all out of whack.

My sense of identity was an even sorrier state. I didn't know which end was up anymore, but I was well aware of the concept that sleeping in would forever be a joke with Olivia in my life.

"Hang on." I yawned as I rubbed more sleep from my eyes. "Hang on," I mumbled to her as I opened my eyes.

Last night was a blur after fucking Eva in that closet. At first, pure shock took hold of me that I'd actually done that. That I'd dragged the Mafia diva into a fucking closet, said all those wicked things to her, and rammed into her like that.

She ran out, and instead of chasing her, I got another drink then asked around where Danicia was. A helpful butler-like man had given me directions. Not only was Olivia sleeping in a guest room where Danicia sat in a chair and watched stand-up comedy acts on her phone, doing her best not to laugh too loudly while she babysat, but they'd also brought up the three duffel bags of my clothes and Olivia's things.

"Hmm." Danicia had given me a clinical once-over when she saw me. "I expect you might be hungover in the morning, so it's just as well I had some things set in the kitchenette over there." She pointed at the counter in the other corner of the room.

I wasn't wasted, but buzzed. Although whether that was from Eva or the alcohol, I couldn't tell.

"Hydrate," she advised as she moved toward the door. "I'll check on you two tomorrow."

I nodded, glad for her help. Some dad I was, letting a virtual stranger watch over my baby. I had a good sense about her, though. She seemed intelligent and trustworthy, and I appreciated her eagerness to assist me in something I felt like I was lacking in.

"If you'll be sticking around, we can set her up for a pediatric checkup, too," she said before she left me.

Now, though, in the morning light, I wondered if Olivia and I would be hanging around for a while. Or at all.

"Good morning," I told Olivia.

She sat in the crib-like bed, peering up at me like she wasn't sure who to expect. After thirteen months of only seeing her mother or the daycare owner, I was a big change. Maybe after last night, she wanted to see Danicia again.

"Or maybe it's not a good morning," I grumbled. Trying to keep a smile on my face, I willed my hangover headache to go away as I reached for her. If I could figure out a natural hold, how to actually carry her without it looking and feeling awkward, I bet I'd be minimally more confident about this fatherhood thing.

But I wasn't. I was an only child, raised by my grandparents. I didn't have younger cousins or anyone with babies to be near. Tessa was my childhood friend, but I never knew her when she was too young. I was woefully unprepared, but I made sure Olivia was secure in my arms as I walked over to the kitchenette.

"Water for me. Milk for you?" The daycare owner who watched

over Olivia until I arrived said that she liked to listen to her talk. Just rambling, or even talking to herself. Hearing people talk was a distraction she swore by, but I wasn't sure when I'd get used to it. I seldom vocalized my thoughts for myself, and doing so now was weird.

"Yeah?" I asked, looking down into her innocent blue eyes. "Milk?"

"Ba-ba." Her small hand patted my chest, and I smiled.

"Bottle?"

She repeated the babble faster, likely her best attempt of saying *bottle*. Once I grabbed it out of the small fridge, she took it and quickly drank.

"I'll get my own," I quipped as I snatched a water bottle. Last night, I had too many of the wrong bottles and glasses, but I was sure that water and some painkillers would erase the remnants of how much I drank.

But not her.

I sat on the couch, letting Olivia lean against me as she had her milk. Stretching back slightly, I yawned again and tried to shove away the thoughts of Eva that trickled in too quickly. Now that I revisited what I'd done last night, I struggled to banish her from my mind.

I'd slept with countless women over the years, but I'd never, ever done something like that. A quickie during a party where I knew next to no one. Calling a woman a slut and being so bossy.

But she liked it.

That was the kicker. Eva had seemed to get hotter and go wild when I degraded her and scolded her about being a brat, diva, and slut.

I drank my water, marveling at how… intense it was. She'd pushed and poked at me so much that I'd snapped. All night, since meeting her, I'd struggled with her antagonistic attitude. That give-and-take nature that formed between us was exciting, and it culminated so quickly in the most final way possible.

With my dick deep inside her warm pussy.

Shit. I rubbed my face and groaned. *I've got to stop thinking about her.* It was done. It was over. Short and sexy. That would be the end of my moment with Eva because there was no way in hell she'd give me her attention again. Not with the way she ran out as soon as we'd come.

Olivia stopped drinking and looked at me. I blinked and stared down at her, unsure whether I should talk or what.

Her bottle, now mostly empty, dropped to her lap as she reached up both hands and rubbed over my face. Starting at my jaw, she pushed her tiny fingers up to my cheek, then back down. She saw me rub my face, and now she thought to do the same.

My lips curled up in a smile, and she did the same, babbling and moving on to patting my cheeks.

As we connected, as I let her touch my face and play, I forgot about my water bottle. It tipped, spilling over my lap and hers. Splashing up into her face was all it took to startle her, not to mention the cold liquid seeping into her clothes.

"Shit. Okay. Okay. Let's clean up." I stood, holding her out so water could drip down. Already, she was fussing and crying, unhappy about being wet and cold. "Sorry. I wasn't paying attention." I brought her over to the bed, holding her against me as I searched for her bag.

She'd need new clothes and whatnot. I'd brought all that she had, but it didn't seem like a lot. Pamela seemed to be a minimalist sort of woman. "Crunchy" was how the daycare owner described her, preferring few toys, simple clothes, and the least amount of traditional baby gear as possible. As I rooted through the bag of Olivia's things, I hated that the smaller bag inside it that held dirty clothes surpassed what was left in the clean pile.

"You need some more things, kid," I told her as I set her on the bed.

I'd asked the daycare owner how to change a diaper when I picked her up, and even that had been a crash course. Googling didn't help much. Watching a tutorial on someone changing a plastic doll was not the same as the hands-on experience of changing a real baby's diaper.

Not to mention getting arms and legs in the right holes.

And a live infant's fussiness.

"Okay. There." The moment I got her in new clothes, I picked her up and held her close while I carried the dirty diaper to the trash. But it seemed she didn't want to be held. "No good?" I asked of her squirming and fussing to get down. "Okay. Now what?" I set her on the floor, watching her crawl and explore.

I nodded and gestured at her to go crawl and explore. "All right. Have fun." Until I could talk to Tessa again and start thinking about where to go and what to do for my and Olivia's future, I'd need to get dressed and figure out how to gather more necessities for her. Clothes, bottles, food, other baby things.

Keeping an eye on Olivia pulling up and walking along the bed and other things in the room, I got dressed and laughed when she plopped onto the carpet. "Not as easy as it looks, huh?" I teased of her trying to take more than a couple of independent steps from whatever she'd pulled up to walk along. She didn't stop, though, determined to get up over and over and keep trying. Once she mastered the balance of walking independently, she'd take off. I was sure of it.

Maybe I'll adjust easier when she's less of a baby and more of a child? I'd never envisioned myself as a dad. While this was all new and I worried I'd struggle to adjust every single day, I was glad that I didn't have to figure out how to be an impromptu parent of an even younger baby.

"Let's go see if we can find Tessa." I picked her up, glad that she didn't protest being held again. When I left the room without her pacifier, she smacked at me and I doubled back, recalling the daycare owner's advice to always have one with her.

Walking through this enormous house felt strange. Last night, I was caught up in the whirlwind of meeting the Constella family members and trying to catch up with Tessa. *And fucking Eva.* Now, in the light of the day without a party held elsewhere in the mansion, it was too quiet. Like we were trespassing, not seeking out my friend. Like I was a soldier on a covert mission to gather intel about a Mafia boss.

Because this is the Mafia's home. I grimaced at the reminder. My ability to navigate the grayness of this situation wouldn't happen quickly. While I would stand by Tessa and make sure she was happy and safe, I wasn't sure I could look the other way with the knowledge that she'd gotten involved with a crime boss.

I turned a corner, wondering if Tessa might be eating breakfast in this huge kitchen-like area or if there was another one somewhere in this maze of a building. The scents of sausage and pancakes filled the air, and Olivia reacted.

"Hmmm. Hmmm." She rubbed her little tummy, too, grinning that she smelled something good.

I laughed lightly as we finally found someone. It seemed that everyone was sleeping in—except the boss.

"Morning," Dante said from the stove. He smiled at Olivia. "You smell the pancakes."

She clapped her hands together, bouncing in my arms.

"Morning." *Weird.* I hadn't personally spent much time with criminal masterminds. I fought in the field, but I wasn't in a ranking to see through one-on-one conversations with leaders. Dante had to be an enemy simply because of the title he held. He was a Mafia boss. But it was strange to see him cooking where he'd have staff to handle it.

He lost his smile for Olivia and frowned at me. Hesitating, as though he wanted to say something, he looked between us.

"What?" Immediately, my guards went up. I didn't trust this man. And I didn't like how he regarded me.

"Can I show you something?" He set the spatula down on the counter and approached.

"Show me what?" I asked.

"How to hold her." He raised his brows as he held his hands out. This gruff Mafia lord wanted to educate me. With holding a baby.

Olivia must not have noticed the tension between me and the older man. While he smiled at her again, she thrust her arms out to go to him. Annoyance filled me that she'd be so trusting of a smiling face. This man had to be a killer. A gangster. God knew what else. I was hung up on the labels and didn't have any reason to trust him—yet.

"Keep one arm over the center of her movements, her hips." Dante held Olivia propped against his side. "And she'll follow how your body moves." He lifted his free hand to grab a mug of coffee and drink it. "Far easier than always holding her with both arms."

I nodded, hating how natural he looked.

"Father to father," Dante added as he handed her back.

"Thanks." *Whatever.* I was sure I'd figure it out on my own eventually. I wasn't a moron.

"Do you think you can set aside whatever biases and judgments you've already formed of me long enough to eat breakfast?" He resumed his spot at the stove, working on the food again.

"I'm not used to associating with the enemy," I said.

He nodded, unbothered. "Noted, Soldier. But the last I checked, the Army didn't have me on their wanted list."

I sat at the island after putting Olivia on the floor to crawl again. Damn, she was fast, but I could multitask in watching her and talking with this man. "The Army might not. But the FBI and CIA?"

Dante shrugged.

"I'm not sure I like the idea of my friend getting involved with a criminal organization."

He arched a brow. "I doubt your opinion would stand between my son and his fiancée."

Dammit. I worried about that too.

"If you could be patient to consider why and how my son met your friend, you might reconsider." He looked at me without any pressure to kowtow to his claim. "In the meantime, help yourself. Nina has specific cravings." He grimaced at the plate of pancakes with pickles on top, all greasy with butter and syrup. "But there is plenty for you and Olivia."

She found him, pulling up to his pants leg. I watched as he stepped away from the stove to pick her up and show her the food.

"Want a bite?" he asked her, also using a sign language gesture to pair his words. "Can you say please?"

"Peas," she replied.

Holy shit. I didn't even know the extent of her vocabulary yet. But he could guess. I couldn't help but be impressed.

I wouldn't mistake this man for anything but the crime lord he was, but I had to consider him in a new light. Unlike me, he was at ease holding a baby. He was generous in offering her food as he cut a small bit of pancake from another plate. He knew how to make it a small bite, then let her hold the utensil with his help so she wouldn't jam it into her mouth.

He was a Mafia lord, but also a generous host. And a father offering me simple advice.

Sometimes... not everything is black and white. Not everything is cut and dry.

And more often than not, looks could be deceiving. I had no doubts the older man holding my daughter and offering her food was a deadly killer, but it seemed that wasn't *all* he was.

"More, please?" he asked her as she made grabby hands for the fork. He did the sign language again. He glanced at me. "Can she have more?"

I nodded. "We haven't eaten yet."

"Help yourself," he offered again before showing Olivia how to sign for *more please*. I watched, curious and guarded, as she figured out the gesture. I got a plate of food for myself, counting on sharing some with her, too.

"Moe peas," she said in her little voice.

I smiled as she grinned, happy that Dante gave her another bite.

"You can have as much as you want," he told her as he brought her back to me. Or maybe he was talking to me.

She settled on my lap, all her focus on the plate of food, and I was quick enough to slide it out of her reach before she smacked her hands on it all.

"Guess it's not too soon to get the child-proof plates and cutlery out," Dante quipped as he set Nina's breakfast on a tray.

Damn. The boss made breakfast himself. He was taking his food to his woman, breakfast in bed. He was at ease with scolding my impatient daughter to ask nicely for another bite.

If I hadn't already known he was a Mafia man, he could have very well looked like a normal guy caring for those around him.

He left us to eat, and while we did, I struggled with figuring out how to interpret who the Constellas really were. Just a ruthless Mafia organization? Or something else?

Because I could hardly fault Tessa for wanting to marry one of them when I was just as quick to fuck one in a closet.

That was just lust. Nothing more. I rolled my eyes, catching myself thinking of her as I cleaned up Olivia after she was done eating.

I wouldn't be duped. This wasn't a hotel. This was a Mafia boss's home and I'd be wise to keep my guard up.

Including around Eva. I wasn't sure who we'd run into next and how else someone might surprise me and make me wonder if I was too rash with my opinions of this family.

But it was far too soon to face Eva again.

6

EVA

While I was a coward to run away from Liam after we had sex in the closet, I refused to admit that I was still a coward to avoid him.

I shouldn't have been stuck with this issue. He came to the engagement party. He saw. And he left. Right? Romeo and Tessa had countless guests over that night, and none of them lingered and stayed as a guest overnight in my uncle's mansion.

But he had. Each time I stopped by the big house where Romeo and Tessa were staying while they dealt with more intense renovations at their house, I spotted Liam walking by. Or bumping into him in the kitchen. Or as he headed upstairs to the guest rooms.

He lingered. He hadn't left yet, clearly. And each time we encountered each other, it was the same act of acting ignorant and dodging each other.

We'd freeze upon seeing each other, then a race would commence, one of seeing who could mask their surprise and annoyance the soonest.

Liam and I weren't acknowledging each other. We didn't speak a word of hello. Nothing. Not a single greeting.

I didn't know *what* to say. He seemed ready to pretend he'd never even met me.

Which was fine. I didn't need to talk to him, and I saw no point in reaching out to him and asking why he was still here. Maybe he and Tessa still wanted to catch up. They were old friends and all. Many guests visited for more than a few days. My uncle even opened up guest rooms for soldiers and members of the family who needed an alternative place to stay. It was that big of a mansion.

Just not big enough for me to forget Liam was there. Somewhere.

"But why is he still here?" I asked Nina one afternoon, a week after the engagement party. We were supposed to be browsing online for more decorations for her baby shower, but she was more interested in searching through baby name lists.

"Liam?" Nina glanced up and shrugged. "Seeing as he just got out of the military, he's catching up."

I furrowed my brow. The military? I wasn't surprised. He had that sort of demeanor and aura. A man of combat. A man of a well-honed body tailored for endurance. That attitude and stiff cockiness. They all suited him, but I was slightly curious about this new fact I could obsess over.

"He was discharged?"

"Recently," Nina answered, not looking up from the baby name lists yet. "I think he was wounded in combat and there is something that would prohibit him from active duty. Or full active duty?" She waved her hand, dismissing it. "I don't remember all that jargon. My dad used to mention duty levels and such, and it always seemed so complex and confusing."

Liam didn't seem wounded or injured. I hadn't seen all of him that night. Actually, I saw next to nothing since we hadn't taken the time to remove our clothes—except my panties.

I slid my tongue along the seam of my closed lips, schooling myself to resist the blush that threatened to bloom.

My panties. Which I left on the damn floor in the closet... Unless he took them.

"Are you all right?" Nina frowned at me, and I flinched.

"Hmm? Yeah. I'm fine."

Not fine. So, so far from fine. Because every time I thought about what that rugged man said and did to me, what I begged for him to do with me…

"You look warm." Nina narrowed her eyes.

"Nah. It's just the humidity in here." While the pool was closed outside, the smaller indoor one in the solarium was just as nice. Neither of us wanted to get back in, preferring to lounge under the windows while our bathing suits dried.

"Oh." Nina didn't push it. If she saw me actually blushing, I'd never hear the end of it. I was too well-known to hide all my emotions.

"Anyway, he's just left the military." Nina sighed, closing her eyes and settling into the reclined chair.

"But how long is he going to stay *here?*" I asked.

The sooner he left, the easier it would be to forget about him. That had to hold true. Because the longer he was around, he was nothing but a forbidden fruit I couldn't want. Close enough to reach, but so far from what I should desire.

"I don't know," Nina said, frustrated. "It's not like he's in the way. He keeps to himself, and—"

"Who's not in the way?" Tessa asked as she entered the solarium, joining us. She looked between me and Nina as she took off her cover up, clearly planning to get into the pool.

"Liam." Nina rolled her eyes. "Miss Uncongeniality over here is asking why he's still visiting."

Tessa huffed. "Leave him be."

Uh, way too late for that piece of advice. He'd told me himself to leave him alone, and that was just a way of throwing fuel onto the fire of wanting him.

"I don't understand why he's got to visit for so long."

"Maybe it's more than a visit," Tessa argued, defensive and curt. She stepped into the heated pool but kept her focus on me.

"He's moving here?" *God, no. No, no, no.* I needed him to go and stop messing with me. He might have said that he'd ruin me as a smug, self-centered man who thought he was God's gift to womankind. But he *had* ruined me, at least in this case of temporary insanity.

I'd caught myself mentally replaying the terse arguments we had, brief though they were. I thought about him before I fell asleep, damning him for challenging me. I slept and experienced illicit dreams of him kissing me and fucking me harder, everywhere. And I would be so damn grateful for a break from wanting him. He'd burrowed in so deep that I couldn't shake my mind from all thoughts of him, and it was grating on my nerves.

"Why?" I blurted the simple question before I could stop myself.

Nina and Tessa both faced me, suspicion clear in their expressions.

"What do you mean, *why*?" Tessa asked. "There's more than enough room here. He's not in your way, in anyone's way."

Oh, au contraire, Tess. He is. He is so totally in my way—mentally.

I was so frustrated with wanting him again that I was half-tempted to leave for an impulsive vacation far, far from here.

A change of scenery would surely cure this stupid fixation, one I had no business having for someone like him, an outsider who didn't seem to care who I was in this organization.

"He's my guest. My friend."

I raked my teeth over my lower lip. "Yeah. I know. I get that. But—"

"No *but*." Tessa narrowed her eyes again, not happy with how I questioned her. She'd struggled with thinking that she fit in with us, that she could be a *real* part of the Constella Family. I bet a lot of that doubt took root when the Giovannis tried to kidnap Nina but dismissed Tessa, claiming she was just a piece of ass to Romeo. How wrong they were. Tessa was irrefutably part of our family, and she belonged with my cousin.

"Liam is as welcome here as anyone else acquainted with the Constella Family. Even though Liam's *my* friend and someone I knew before I met you all, he's just as worthy of staying here."

I looked away, not wanting to make this an issue about her importance here. If she wanted to invite a guest to stay here at any of the Constella properties, then she could. I didn't care. I just wanted *him* gone, to remove the temptation so I could go back to being my usual sort of miserable.

"He is welcome to stay for as long as he wants," Nina said.

"And if that takes a while, until he figures out what he's going to do next, then so be it," Tessa concluded.

"Until he figures out what to do?" I asked, shaking my head. "Why? Because he just got out of the military?" A memory clicked. Before the engagement party, I walked through the kitchen and overheard these two women talking about someone getting a job. I pointed at Tessa. "Is that what you two were talking about before the party? That someone needs a job?"

Tessa nodded. "Yes. A job and a place to stay." She glanced at Nina. "I don't see why he can't just work for the family, but he's been... stubborn about that."

Oh, fuck no. If Liam were recruited as a soldier, I'd be stuck with this forbidden attraction for good. "Stubborn how?"

"He's too quick to label us all as Mafia gangsters. Automatically, the bad guys—oh, hey!" Nina brightened as someone else entered the solarium. "Time for some fun in the water."

A tiny little voice of glee reached my ears. It sounded an awful lot like a baby, but there weren't any kids around here.

Frowning, I slowly turned to see Liam stride into the room. In his arms was proof of my ignorance.

There was a kid in the house, and not the baby still in Nina's belly.

He held one, a sweet, smiling, golden-haired toddler. She clapped and kicked as she saw Tessa in the water.

"Are you..."

A father? That child had to be his. The family resemblance was so obvious. But...

"Are you shitting me?" I asked, stunned and stupefied as I took in the package look of Liam and his daughter. Seeing him in a tight T-shirt and swim shorts was mouth-watering enough. But seeing him with a baby?'

Oh, fuck no.

"What..." I shook my head, having the slightest clarity of mind to stop gawking. "What is this?"

A joke?

Liam glanced at me coolly. If I hadn't already been staring at him, I might have missed the subtle way he faltered, almost like a double-take at seeing me in my bikini. He reverted to that stony stoicism, though, returning his attention to the toddler in his arms. "Want to swim with Aunt Tess?"

Oh, fuck me. This was too much. He was gorgeous enough, so ripped and hardened in that perfectly masculine manner of melting my panties off. But knowing he was a dad?

I was mush, unable to tear my stare from them.

She was so small and secure in his big, strong arms. Something about the image of this rough-and-tumble man being so gentle and protective of that innocent little girl made me see him in another light. That he wasn't just the dirty-talking, smug, expert lover who could rock my world in a quickie. He was also a parent. A caregiver. Someone who gave his all for someone else.

Dammit. I'd never cared much for the expression of ovaries exploding, but I understood it now. Maybe it was hormones. Maybe it was stupidity. But seeing Liam with a baby was a potent tease.

"Eva, meet Olivia," Tessa said, smirking at me. She smiled widely, entertained with how surprised I was to see that Liam had a baby girl. "Isn't she the cutest?"

I numbly nodded, overwhelmed with this new fact I'd need to dissect about the man I shouldn't want.

"She's darling," I replied as I hurried to scramble off my chair. "Really... darling."

I turned and escaped the room, unable to face that man, especially with how much hotter he looked as a father.

7

LIAM

Eva ran out of the solarium, and I wasn't strong enough to resist staring at her as she went. I'd held that luscious ass in my hands once, and it was a mistake I refused to repeat.

Seeing her in that black bikini was torture. It was as close as I'd ever get to seeing her uncovered, and it was both a blessing and a damnation. A blessing because I could now have the visual to fantasize about. But a damnation because I shouldn't be dreaming about having her again.

Even if I had ample time to lie around and enjoy casual sex with her, we were ill-fated to not get along. She was too prickly. I was too prejudiced.

That prejudice was fading, though, and it irked me how much these Constellas chipped away at the biases I'd held against them from day one.

"They're in the fucking Mafia, though," I said on a call with an old army friend. Ethan was one of the good ones I'd toured with. He retired a few years ago, but we'd stayed in touch. In fact, he was one of the men I considered reaching out to when I debated not signing up for more of the army. Located in Brooklyn, he was sort of nearby.

After a week of being in Dante's mansion and catching up with Tessa, though, I was wondering if I should be hasty to leave.

I didn't want to mooch, and Tessa and the others never implied that I was, but I felt comfortable to stay here with Olivia, where we were guarded and safe, until I figured out what else I could do.

This morning at breakfast, where I encountered Dante again, he posed the possibility of my working for the family.

"So?" Ethan replied.

I cringed as I paced in the guest room. Olivia was napping, but if I kept my voice low, I wouldn't disturb her. I still glanced at her as I walked by, both to check that she was resting and just in the marvel that she was mine and I was a father. It had yet to fully sink in. "So?" I replied. "They're criminals."

"Yeah, but in the scheme of all the good and evil out there in the world, who gives a shit?"

"That's blunt."

"It is, but it's true. You take any organization in the world, any entity of power, and you know it's corrupt. Or it had been. Or it soon will be."

"I know." He had valid points. No government or leadership on the face of this earth was free from corruption. Religions, clubs, cults, gangs. They all had equal likelihood of succumbing to one evil or another. "It's part of human nature."

"Yeah. Damn right. you get a group of people together, and they'll figure out a way to hoard power. We were pawns in the government's power, serving how we did. It's no different from any organized crime family. Just… domestic, I suppose."

"True, but it's not an easy jump to consider." I hadn't told him any specifics. I didn't mention the Constella name. I wasn't stupid. But after Dante's job offer to join as a Constella soldier, I wanted a fellow serviceman's opinion.

"At least it's a respected crime family wanting you on board." Ethan's chuckle was dry and raspy, just like it was when we fought together. He hadn't changed a bit. "Everyone fears the Mafia. Not like it's some lowlife MC or biker gang trying to pull you in."

I snorted a laugh. "Yeah, right." I did have a motorcycle. It was supposed to be delivered whenever I had an address to ship it to. It was a purchase that better suited my nomadic life. Without a house to keep up while I was touring, I could store my bike far easier.

Not anymore. Now that I had Olivia, I had to do all the typical adult shit that everyone did when they settled. I needed a home, an address for my bike to come to and also to serve as a residence for me and my daughter. To obtain that, I needed a job, a source of income before I considered draining my savings from my time in the army.

"Consider it," Ethan advised. "Sleep on it. You're welcome to bring your kiddo and crash here. My grandson stays during the summers, but there's plenty of room."

"I appreciate it." I disconnected and mulled over what he'd said. It was all valid. Any powerful group was prone to a bad rep from one source or another. The military I'd served for had its own select few who were corrupt and selfish.

Human nature. That was what it boiled down to. But I wasn't making a choice for just myself. I had Olivia to consider. If I signed up for a job with the Constella Family, I'd risk her losing her only family. If anything happened to me on the job, she'd have no one.

But what else would I do? After my career in the army, something in security or law enforcement was all that I'd be trained for. All I'd be interested in. A desk job wasn't in the cards. Another trade would require me to learn it.

I stopped and watched Olivia sleep, her tiny chest rising and falling with her cute face so relaxed in the bliss of sleep. It still hit me so hard that she was mine, the product of a one-night stand. I couldn't remember much about Pamela. That was how insignificant she was in my memories, and likewise from her perspective about me if she never felt the need to tell me that I had a daughter. Yet, she'd given me the most important person in the world.

I know I'm still figuring it out, Liv. I'm learning as I go. But I swear I will always try to do my best for you.

Which meant getting a damn job and a place to live.

I groaned lightly and ran my hands through my hair as I paced again. It should be so simple. Say yes. Join the Constellas. Take up Dante's offer to stay in one of the many guest houses they had. But I struggled, anyway.

Tessa had been spending a lot of time with me in the week since her engagement party. Over and over, she relayed how she'd met Romeo. That he'd killed her rapists. And when he'd saved her from threats.

On one hand, I was glad for the man avenging my old friend. On the other, though, I was worried about how close danger clung to them.

Later, when Nina joined one of our conversations, she explained how she and Dante had met. That her loser brother lost her in a bet and Dante rescued her.

Both their stories helped me understand that they were capable of doing good, but I was too guarded to be convinced that quickly.

"Knock, knock." Nina whispered it after she gently rapped on my door and opened it. She peeked inside, smiling at me.

"Oh, hey," I said, letting her in. As if I had to let her in. This was her home. I appreciated that she respected my space, though. It was getting hard to remember that I was a guest with how they made me feel included. "She's still napping."

"Oh." She pouted. "I was hoping we could play."

I laughed once. "With what?" I shook my head at how Pamela went out of her way to deprive Olivia of any toys. Each parent would have their own style, it seemed, and I was not a crunchy sort of guy. There was nothing wrong with toys and actual books with fantastical creatures in them.

"Well, we had a blast in the kitchen with the pots and spoons yesterday." She grinned, stopping me from walking out of the room. "I really appreciate that you're letting me babysit her. It's practice for me." She placed her hand on her belly.

"As if you won't be a perfect mom," I teased. While I knew Nina long ago because she was Tessa's friend, it was nice to befriend her as an adult now. She'd offered to watch Olivia while I went to the store for some necessities, and I got the impression that this was as good for her as it was for me and Olivia. "Thanks again." I stopped at the door. "Wait. Can I borrow a car?"

"Yeah. I think Franco's downstairs. He'll find you something." She smiled and sat near the crib where Liv slept.

I headed down to the first floor, finding both Franco and Romeo. I did my best not to smirk or cling to my guardedness around them, but it was hard to lose that edge of defensiveness. Romeo was a lethal man, a killer, and not just on the battlefield like I had been. Franco was just as deadly.

Here, though, they deceived me, smiling and looking laidback as I came down the stairs.

"Hey, just who I was hoping to talk to," Franco said as he spotted me.

"Oh, yeah?"

Romeo nodded. "My father told us that he asked whether you'd like to work for the family." He stuck his hands in his pockets and tilted his head to the side. While he didn't look intimidating and wasn't pressuring me, I felt the weight of expectation.

I grimaced and rubbed the back of my neck. "I don't know…"

Franco shook his head. "You'd fit right in."

"You check out," Romeo added.

I grunted, annoyed at this intrusion of privacy. "Looked into me, huh?" I crossed my arms.

Romeo nodded while Franco smiled. "Do you think we'd be so stupid as to let a stranger stay in this house without a security clearance?"

"No. And I don't blame you, but—"

"And do you think I would be careless with my fiancée's life to allow a stranger near her?" Romeo asked.

No. And I'd be pissed if you slacked in protecting her.

I sighed.

"What's your biggest concern?" Franco asked.

"Because it's not every day we find a trained fighter like you. With sniper abilities too," Romeo said.

"It's a big shift. Going from the military, to civilian, to… Mafia."

"You don't seem like the sort of person to be hung up on labels," Romeo countered. "At least not when Tess describes you as the guy who rolls so well with punches."

I shrugged. "It's just different is all. Besides, after leaving one institution, I'm reluctant to join another and be a dime-a-dozen employee for a big organization again."

Franco held up his hands. "Hey, no pressure. But please think about it."

"We're here to talk about the offer whenever you want to discuss it," Romeo said.

"I appreciate that." I did. I was grateful for a hell of a lot that they'd offered me in this last week alone. "I will think about it." I intended to, not only because I had to provide for Olivia but because I was slowly getting tempted with the security I could have here—when I wasn't in danger on the frontlines. "But before I do, is there a car I can borrow?" I faced Franco. "Nina said I should ask you for a ride."

"I can drop you off," Romeo offered. "I'm on my way out."

"Thanks, but I was hoping to make a few stops. I'm past due getting Olivia some things."

"Ah." Franco nodded. "I'm sure we can find you something."

Romeo shook his head and pointed behind me. "Don't trouble him with a car, finding parking and all. Eva can take him out."

"I can what?" Eva snapped, coming closer from the entrance to the kitchen where she'd come from. She barely spared me a glance.

"No. No, that's not necessary." Fuck no. Anything but forcing me to deal with the icy brat.

"Yeah. You can help get Liam where he needs to stop. You're used to navigating the city," Romeo said.

"Why me?" she sassed, smirking. "We have tons of drivers who could do the same thing."

I shook my head. "Really. No. I'll figure something else out."

"Eva. Stop being a pain. Help the man out, huh?" Romeo raised his brows, likely confused about why we were both shooting down his idea to volunteer Eva to help me.

Franco was no help. He grinned, amused.

"I'm not here to be a mooch." I stepped back. "It's fine. I'll figure out something easier."

Eva narrowed her eyes at me. "Are you implying that I'm difficult?"

"I think… you're proving that you are without any help from me."

Her jaw dropped. "I'm not difficult."

Romeo and Franco shared a look.

"Just… never mind." I turned, desperate to be further from the woman I couldn't stop thinking about day and night. Her insistence to avoid me was telling enough. I wasn't alone in wanting to keep this distance between us. The tension was still there, raging and building with pent-up energy and attraction. A storm was brewing, and it seemed so much safer to keep a buffer of space from her. Because the only alternative was to reach out for her and show her how much I'd missed her since I'd taken her into that closet. It was agony seeing her and knowing she was off-limits.

"No. I'll take you."

"I said never mind—"

She growled, grabbing my arm. "And I said let's go."

8

EVA

Romeo knew exactly what he was doing, volunteering me to drive Liam around. He'd heard me complaining about Liam being here and doing nothing, just a lazy guest. It was just one way that I'd brainstormed to get the man away, but my cousin twisted it all. He'd tossed my complaint back in my face, implying that I hadn't been doing anything lately. Suggesting that I chauffeur Liam was merely adding fuel to the fire, rubbing salt in the wound.

Ass.

That was the only reason I relented and agreed to spend time with the one man I'd rather avoid for the sake of my sanity. It was why, ten minutes later, I was buckled into my SUV while he rode next to me. I hated being a passenger princess. I loved the independence of driving. I wasn't ever truly independent, always with guards nearby, but I preferred being behind the wheel myself.

"You didn't have to take me," Liam groused, staring out the window.

"I know I didn't have to. No one makes me do anything I'd rather avoid."

Shit. Fuck. I shouldn't have said that.

"Really." Liam faced me, deadpan. "Then I've been reading you wrong all along. It seemed to me that you'd rather walk over hot coals than have my company."

"Just shut up." I didn't want him calling me out for avoiding him. I didn't want him to point out that I'd run from him after that closet incident, either.

"Pull over. I'll call an Uber or something."

"No." I pressed the locks to double-check they were on.

"Why? Why force yourself to put up with me?"

Because I can't stop thinking about you!

"Why force me to put up with you, for that matter?" He shook his head. "I'm sure you've got better things to do than drive me around."

I narrowed my eyes, keeping my focus on the road. "What the hell does that mean?"

"It means exactly what I said. Don't put yourself out on my account. I'm sure you've got a busy day of acting like a spoiled brat."

"Are you suggesting I don't have a job? Nothing to do?" That *really* burned. If I hadn't been brooding and moping about not having a purpose or something to concentrate on, his words would've gone in one ear and out the other. But I had been thinking about that, wishing I had a job to preoccupy myself.

"Don't put words in my mouth."

"Don't try to insinuate and put words in my mouth, either."

He scowled, confused with my comeback that didn't really make sense. "The only thing I'd think about putting in your mouth is—" He caught himself, tilting his head to the side and squeezing his eyes shut. "No. I'm not going there. *We're* not going there."

My cheeks heated up. I felt the flush spreading over my face. As odd as it was to be blushing, I couldn't get past the blatant appeal of what he'd stopped himself from finishing.

He wanted to cram his big cock into my mouth? To fuck me there? *Please. Fuck yes. Please.*

"Why are you like this?" he asked, looking out the window again.

"Spoiled?" I huffed, needing this bitter bickering more than the lead-in to seductive thoughts like sucking on him. "I'm not spoiled."

"Yeah. Sure. If you grew up in a home like that mansion, with multiple pools, staff, and no job, I fail to see how you escaped being spoiled."

"I'm not," I insisted. "It's all part of the projection of power. The Constella Family is wealthy and influential, and with those conditions, we represent that status of life."

"Fine. Whatever." I waved it off. "I wouldn't understand it. I grew up modestly. Like Tessa."

"She never calls me spoiled." I hated that his opinion of me mattered so much. I truly wasn't, though. "I may wear designer and have professional stylists, but it's because that's the position I am in. I am expected to look the part of a Mafia princess—"

He chuckled wryly. "Princess. Yeah, you act like one."

"But the things and materials don't matter."

Looking me up and down, he studied me. "You'd be just as happy to be poor and without all the leisure?"

I sighed. *With the right person, yes.* "It's never been an option. I was born into this life."

"And it molded you into an icy bitch."

At a red light, I glowered at him. "You're an ass."

He shrugged. "I'm just calling it like it is." Shifting in his seat to face me, he crossed his arms and settled in to chat. "Does Tessa say you're an icy bitch?"

"No." *But she did admit that I was a bratty diva once.*

"Does Nina?"

"Not really." *But Uncle Dante called me out about not welcoming her at first.*

"So it's just me. I'm the lucky one to get the difficult version of you."

"No. I—" I pressed my lips together and exhaled hard through my nose. "Maybe."

He huffed. "Nice."

"You inspire me to be combative."

He shook his head. "No. It's not just me. I overhear you arguing with everyone in that house."

"I'm not a pushover."

"Except in a closet. With me."

Oh, damn you. I cleared my throat and refused to respond.

"You bicker with Romeo."

"He's more like a brother than a cousin. Siblings bicker."

He smirked. "And Franco. I've caught you arguing with him."

"Fine!" I flung my hand in the air. "I'm argumentative."

"Why? Why do you ice everyone out?" When I didn't reply, he added, "Why act like such a bitch to me but want to drive me around? Make up your mind, Eva. I'm not pursuing you. I'm not asking you for a damn thing."

That's the problem. He dismissed me. He was fine with cutting me out of his life while I needed more than a closet quickie. Liam Gray was simply too different, too far from what I was used to that I couldn't be done with him yet.

"Because I've been raised that way." I sighed. "I've only had Uncle Dante. He's a tough man, and he's raised me to be tough." I also never had much of a maternal role model to soften me out. With Uncle Dante's expectations, to raise me as a strong woman in the Mafia, I grew up knowing I'd need to be firm. And at times, that equaled being cold.

"Not that tough." He almost smiled, looking back out the window. "He surprises me the most. Every morning, I see him in the kitchen making breakfast. I mean, the guy is loaded. He's got chefs, maids, housekeepers. But he's the one in there personally making his fiancée breakfast in bed."

"That's what impresses you the most about Uncle Dante?" I almost laughed. It was so simple.

"It's what makes me think he's more than a cold-blooded Mafia boss."

I rolled my eyes. "He goes out of his way because he's that obsessed with taking care of Nina. It's all her doing."

He furrowed his brow. "He worries that someone would poison her?"

"No!" Now I did laugh. We all trusted the staff on the properties we owned. They were like extensions of family. "He wants her to know that he cares. That if he's bringing her breakfast in bed, that she can know he made it, thinking of her."

"Huh."

"Where to?" I asked, enjoying this chance to be with just him. To talk. I wanted him, but this was nice too.

He typed in an address on the navigation. "Target."

"Why not have it delivered?"

He shrugged. "I've never shopped for this kind of stuff before. I figured it might make more sense to see it in person." He glanced at me, brows raised again. "If you're too busy, I'll find another ride."

I narrowed my eyes at him. "Are you trying to get rid of me?"

He shook his head, but the slow, appreciative look he gave me suggested he'd rather do something else with me.

"I said I'd drive you. And I will. Not because I don't have anything else to do."

"Suit yourself. And I'm hardly in any position to judge you for being unemployed. I am too."

"By choice?"

He shook his head. "No. I need to figure something out soon." After he shifted in his seat, I realized he was uncomfortable. Not necessarily physically, but maybe with the idea of finding work. "Although your uncle wants me to work for him now."

"So I've heard." I knew he had to notice me glancing at him, but he didn't take the bait and make eye contact before the light turned green. "Are you considering it?"

"I'm not crazy about the idea of being one of many working for another institution." He shrugged. "I wanted out of the military to do something else for my life."

"To march to the beat of your own drum? Something like that?"

"Yeah, I guess. I was just tired of the same old, tours one after the other. But that was before I found out about Olivia."

I'd been dying to learn more about how he came to be a father. I hadn't asked Tessa or anyone else out of the fear that I'd look too curious about Liam. "If you were overseas for so long, how...?" I shook my head.

"Olivia was the product of a one-night stand. Her mother was someone I met in a bar while I was serving. And she passed away from a drunk driving accident."

"I'm sorry to hear that."

"Me too. I wasn't close. I don't think she even gave me her last name when we hooked up. But she apparently knew who I was, enough that she had me listed as an emergency contact at the daycare she dropped Olivia off at."

"Wow." That seemed so impersonal.

"It was just a hookup." He rubbed his face. "Cheryl, the daycare owner, contacted me and explained it all. According to her, Pamela thought I was a military man who wouldn't have the time for a baby, and she'd rather raise her how she saw fit."

"That's still cruel not to inform you. She's your child."

He nodded. "I understand her perspective."

"*Is* she your child?" Olivia looked like him, but still, I had to wonder.

"Yes. Cheryl insisted on a paternity test when I showed up. She watched over Olivia until I came. It was either I man up and take my daughter or let her go through into the system, and I'd be damned if I did that to my flesh and blood. My grandparents stepped up to raise me when my parents bailed on me, and I couldn't consider abandoning *my* kid, even if she was a complete surprise."

Now it made sense, how overwhelmed Liam looked all the time. He'd had a lot put on him quickly and so unexpectedly.

Once we arrived at Target, we went through the list that I'd noted on my phone.

"How can she not have *any* toys?" I asked, trying to puzzle out what some of them did. All the labels were helpful, indicating what ages the items were intended for and what skills they helped to foster, like fine-motor movement or eye coordination.

"Cheryl said Pamela was a very strict vegan, 'crunchy', and eco-friendly parent. No plastic at all. No artificial anything, at all." He shrugged, looking as lost as I felt at the array of toys and gadgets.

"So... what, wood blocks?" I picked a package up.

"I guess?" He grabbed a stuffed animal of a dog. "This can't be so bad?" He peered at the label.

"Maybe next time, you should bring Olivia shopping and let her point at what she wants."

He cringed. "Fuck."

A parent pushing a shopping cart gasped and covered her toddler's ears. "Mind your language!" she scolded him.

I covered my hand to block my gesture from the kid and flipped off the woman. "Mind your own business."

Liam smirked and shook his head. "I'm assuming Olivia's too young to repeat what I say."

"Yet," I added.

"Yeah. Yet. But that reminds me that I need a car seat thing. And a stroller. And…" He whooshed out a long breath. "This will take a while."

I held my hand out. "Let me see that list."

He gave me his phone and I skimmed the list. "I can help."

His expression was unreadable, but I noted the hint of disbelief. "You? Because you're an expert with thirteen-month-olds?"

"No." I crossed my arms. "No more than you are. We can figure it out together."

And so we did. We shopped and deciphered the best we could. He seemed quicker at understanding all the safety abbreviations and icons on the stroller, high chair, and other odds and ends, but he deferred to me about the color coordination and practicality of clothes and outfits.

For hours—most of the afternoon and into the evening—we teamed up against our cluelessness and tried to get all the basics for Olivia. As long as we didn't talk about ourselves or get too far off on a tangent of why we wouldn't budge on any one of our particular opinions, it wasn't that hard to get along with him. To partner up. To while away the day.

"Damn. We missed dinner," I said as we took all the purchases to the car after a couple of hours at another store.

He frowned, glancing around as we walked to the car. "Yeah. Sorry."

I furrowed my brow. "Okay. That's not the first time you've acted like this. What's wrong?"

I'd noticed him getting tense and more alert when we went from one store to the next. I dismissed it as nothing more than being super aware of his surroundings, but I wasn't imagining how much closer he stood to me now.

"I think..." He turned his head slightly to the left but his eyes tracked something to the right.

"Huh?" I looked forward, trying to understand what he could be looking at in the reflections of any of the car windows in this lot.

"I—" He growled, reacting too quickly to finish speaking. With a firm shove down, he covered me and forced me to duck under him.

I dropped beneath him and sucked in a breath to hold as his hard arm snaked around my waist.

"Stay down!" He rolled as he ordered it.

We slammed to the ground together, stopping the momentum of our roll against a parked car. With him shouting in my ear, it was harder to hear the shot from afar.

As I looked up, sheltered by his body over mine, I stared at the bullet hole in the window of the car.

The bullet that would've gone right through my head if he hadn't pushed me to safety.

9

LIAM

"Are you okay?" I turned slightly, out of breath from the adrenaline rush. Cupping Eva's face between my hands, I stared into her eyes.

She gazed right back at me, those dark brown orbs clear but showing fear. Alarm. I'd scared her, tucking her low and rolling her to safety. But she saw the bullet hole in the glass. I didn't have to spell a single thing out for her to make her understand.

Eva was well aware of the danger.

She was likely used to it, and that thought pissed me off.

"Are you hurt?" I asked, concerned that she could've been wounded in that sudden fall. I wasn't a small man, and I'd made sure to cover all of her in case the shooter tried again.

"Yes." She swallowed hard and nodded. The motion prompted me to lower my hands from her face, but I didn't retreat. I remained crouching low, still blocking her with my body.

The moment was tense, as were any instances sharp on the tail of a life-or-death situation.

All day, I'd struggled to resist that gnawing inner sense that someone was following us. That a person was watching us. I posed no threat. I wasn't a target. I had no enemies. But she would—as a Constella.

"I'm not hurt, Liam," she said, firmly and sincerely.

I nodded, catching my breath like she was from the rush. "Okay." But I made no move to stand yet. Even though the guards were running up to us, no doubt alerted to the active shooter, I couldn't let her leave this bubble, this tight proximity of our bodies close together, mine protecting hers. With the sharp tension of real and present danger in the mix, I couldn't snap out of this soldier mode, this overprotective mindset, and return to the almost easygoing comradery we'd forged while we shopped.

"Miss Constella," a guard said as he darted up to us.

"Are you all right?" another said, flanking us on the other side.

I'd dismissed them all day. I'd noticed them, and I witnessed that they were up to the task of being members of her security detail. They didn't crowd in on us, though, giving us space.

Space that made no difference with a sniper. I stood, keeping myself between Eva and the direction where I'd spotted the sniper in the reflections of windows and mirrors. One look over my shoulder proved the lone shooter was gone from the rooftop he'd shot from, but I scanned around us in a three-sixty, anyway. These Constella guards couldn't have helped her from a distance. It was only because I'd been walking with her that I could act in time.

Fuck. I shook my head at the webbed glass that stayed intact around the bullet hole. She'd come this close. Hell, *I* had come that close. We'd risked death today, and that was a sobering thought to chase away everything else.

"Yes, yes." Eva nodded as the guards checked her over. "I'm fine. He covered me."

Both men looked at me, and a third in the distance spoke into his phone. A small crowd began to gather, and as I scoped the parking lot again, I realized that the security men for this shopping area would no doubt be coming by soon. If someone hadn't called in an active shooter yet, they would any second now.

"You don't..." I rubbed my face, aggravated by this incident. Just when I wanted to lower my guard and do something as simple as shop with Eva, laughing at our mutual confusion of not knowing what to buy a thirteen-month-old girl who was too advanced for baby rattles but too young for more intense gadgets and gizmos, this bullshit had to happen.

Because she's not a simple woman living an ordinary life. She's a Mafia princess, protected and raised to be tough in a violent world of crime and power.

"You don't want the cops to come, right?" I felt stupid to ask, but it was prudent to mention it.

"Let's go," one guard said, an older man who seemed to be in charge.

"We'll head back to the house," Eva said, her face tight with weariness but putting up a brave front to hide her uneasiness.

"Yeah." I nodded, hating that she had to be so used to this. That this was routine for her. She didn't deserve to be a target. She shouldn't have to fear for her life—ever.

But as I got into the car and noticed her fingers shaking as she started the engine, I knew she wasn't actually alone in this. Guns were everywhere. Crazy people could kill anytime in schools, malls, concerts. This shit happened everywhere. And if she weren't protected, she could be in worse conditions as an abused woman unable to escape a violent partner. It was all feasible, but having a sniper on her back? That was wrong, too wrong.

The drive back to the house was quiet. I fumed, angry that she had to be in this position. She drove with utmost concentration, furrowing her brow as she steered. Every so often, she checked her mirrors, likely anxious to know the guards were right behind her.

"He ran," I said after a long stretch of quiet. I couldn't take this silence. "The sniper took off."

She nodded. I noticed through my peripheral vision. "They're always out there."

It was my turn to nod, but I did so while I contemplated the truth of what she said. If I hadn't been with her, would another guard be on her to protect her? "How often does this happen?"

"Not... Not often." She sighed, glancing at me and seeming nervous. If not about what happened, then maybe about my reaction. "Security has been high lately. Another Family and organization have been targeting us. Usually, things are calmer—within reason. Attacks in daylight, in public places like that, are not the norm."

"Because of the risk of killing civilians?"

Shit. As soon as the words left my lips, I realized what I'd said. I said *civilians* in reference to everyone else in that parking lot. But *I* was supposed to be a civilian.

Funny that I couldn't remember to act like it. The need to defend and protect wasn't something I'd ever switch off, and I wondered if I was being selfish not to join the Constellas.

If I weren't there... If she was shot...

I didn't want to consider it. My feelings about Eva were complicated, but I damn well didn't want her to be harmed. I cared. I cared far too much and didn't want to admit it, but I felt like I was stuck in a position where I shouldn't, that I didn't belong with her, with these people she called her family.

Fuck. It was all getting so twisted up. She was supposed to be nothing more than a woman I had a quickie with, a stranger I could consider more like a friend after we shopped and fell into an easier companionship. While we focused on buying things for Olivia and just talking, getting to know more about each other, we could shelve the intense magnetism and deny the chemistry that hadn't faded between us.

But now I was stuck worrying about her safety.

And wanting to be the one to protect her.

No. This can't be the answer. Recruit with the Mafia straight out of the military? It's nonsense.

When we arrived, Eva turned off the engine and glanced at me. "Someone will bring your things in. Uncle Dante will expect you to report to him about this."

She sounded resigned, but I couldn't help but wonder what she was really thinking and feeling.

"Yeah. I figured as much," I mumbled as I got out of the car. The need to make sure she was all right was still ingrained in me. I followed right behind her on the short walk inside.

Once we entered, Romeo approached. "Liam?"

"Yeah, yeah." I nodded, glancing back toward Eva to check once more that she was all right. It was a scare, and even if she was used to the possibility of danger, that didn't mean she couldn't be traumatized.

She was already gone, heading further into the house.

I sighed, hating that the privacy and companionship we'd shared was gone. It had been shattered in that moment of danger, and I wasn't sure when to count on fighting for that middle ground with her again. If we weren't avoiding each other, we were arguing. Something in the middle was a nice break.

Following Romeo into an office, I braced myself to debrief the Mafia men. It was so similar to being in the army, this expectation to report in and be brief and clear with details.

Strangely, it felt normal. Good. Like I'd never stopped being an identity of defense, just in another place and using my training and skills in a different way.

Answering to Dante wasn't a hardship, either. He wasn't a hard ass like my supervisors in the military. He sat in a chair, alert but not barking orders just because he was my superior in rank.

"What happened?" It was a blunt, direct, and simple question I could answer freely.

"I thought we were being followed throughout the day. I noticed it more when we entered or exited the stores. At first, I thought it was a matter of getting used to the guards tailing us." I looked at all three men—Dante, Romeo, and Franco—to make sure they understood. "They weren't slacking. They were attentive and alert on duty as her bodyguards. In the parking lot, I scanned the perimeter and detected movement in a reflection."

Franco nodded. "You know what to look for, huh?"

Dante cleared his throat. "We've looked into your background, Liam. Tessa can vouch for you, but that only goes so far."

I dismissed him with a wave. "I'm not surprised. I'd be more surprised if a man in your position *didn't* look into anyone he let stay in his house."

He nodded. "Go on."

"That's pretty much it. I spotted a sniper and calculated which angle he'd be shooting from. Then I covered Eva and made sure she stayed down until backup came."

Romeo raised his brows. "Very impressive, knowing which way to dive. Not every man would know."

I huffed a dry laugh. "Yeah, well, I've been there and done that."

"Yet you won't consider joining us? Working for me?" Dante asked, serious and not wheedling.

"I have been thinking about it." *And I'm thinking about it a lot more since I just jumped into action to keep Eva safe.* "And I'll continue to think about your offer. But it's not a simple decision of choosing an employer. Now that I've got to adjust—quickly—to being a father and figuring out how to balance being a single parent, on top of leaving a career that I'd been in without pause for a long time…"

Franco patted my back. "Think about it some more."

"Regardless of your choice of being one of the men in our organization," Dante said as he stood and shook my hand, "I appreciate your quick thinking and selflessness to protect my niece. She's the daughter I never had, and I am grateful for your unflinching instinct to keep her safe."

"No problem." It wasn't. Keeping others safe was simply part of who I was. The only problem that could complicate things was if I got caught up with the desire to be the only man she looked to for protection.

I had no right wanting Eva. I shouldn't have been thinking about her this much. Hell, I was wrong to ever pull her aside and fuck her, no matter how much she'd wanted me.

Working for her uncle would be another facet of complications between us. Sleeping with the woman the boss considered his daughter? That was only asking for trouble.

"And it, uh," Franco said, stalling as he rubbed his chin and glanced at me, then Romeo and Dante, "it goes without saying that you don't need to call the cops or anything..."

I rolled my eyes. "I think I picked up on the fact that you police yourselves and handle this side of justice."

Romeo nodded. "Correct. We have a few individuals we suspect might be behind this. And we will investigate this incident accordingly."

I should hope so. I nodded and left, knowing these men would have the resources to look into who put a hit on Eva. If Dante killed a dozen bikers to rescue Nina and if Romeo killed Tessa's rapists, it seemed like a given that they would extend that same executioner attitude toward whoever wronged Eva.

And it was strange how much their brand of law and order was starting to make sense. I couldn't tell if it was my call with Ethan—who considered doing hit jobs—or if it was something else, something like... loyalty.

I shook my head, thinking about it all as I headed to the guest room.

When I got there and didn't see any sign of Olivia, I frowned and glanced at my phone. Nina would've called if she took her anywhere.

Instead of a message from Nina, I saw a text from Tessa in a group chat she'd started with me and Nina. The picture of them holding my daughter in the water reassured me that she was in good hands.

Tessa: *Auntie Nina and Auntie Tessa wanted some more pool time with Liv!*

She looked happy—all of them did. Both women were all smiles in the selfie, and Liv looked content to splash around.

I sighed, glad that she was accounted for. I didn't want to depend on them too much, and I hadn't been. All week, I was with Olivia, getting both of us more used to each other in our new little family. Today, though, I was damned grateful for the babysitting.

Even though I was "home" or back again, I wanted a moment to shower and decompress after the danger. I pulled my shirt off as I padded toward the bathroom and turned the shower on. Kicking off my shoes came next, but I didn't get further than that.

With my hands on my jeans, the zipper halfway undone, someone knocked on the door. I bit back a groan that it might be Tessa and Nina with Olivia already, since that text was from ten minutes ago.

So much for having a moment to myself and relaxing.

I headed toward the door, realizing my shower would have to wait. But it wasn't my babysitters bailing on me and returning Olivia. Instead, I accepted the surprise of finding Eva there.

She pressed her lips together and stared up at me. If she had something to say, she was trying her best not to blurt it out. Under her attention, I realized I'd paused halfway through undressing.

I raised my brows, wondering if she was more shaken by the incident than she'd revealed. Perhaps she wanted to check on me after my report to Dante.

"I..." She shook her head, cutting herself off. Maybe she needed to search a little more for her words and phrase her thoughts.

When she stepped in, forcing me further into the room as she closed the door behind her, it seemed that she wasn't in the mood to talk at all.

She reached for me, sliding her hand up my bare chest until she gripped the back of my neck. As she pulled me down, I let myself get lost in the heated look she gave me from beneath her hooded lids.

"I..." She furrowed her brow, staring at me with such bold need. Damn, she was sexy when she was aroused and desperate.

"Me too." I wanted her just as badly, but I was determined to fight it.

Yeah, right.

We leaned in together, meeting in a crushing kiss.

10

EVA

Liam made a sound as I kissed him back, sealing our lips together. It was instinct, something like a grunt and a moan and a sexy exhale all at once. I didn't know how to define it, but hearing the proof of how much my kiss impacted him turned me on.

Too quickly, before I could fall further into the spell of desire that kissing him built hotter, he pulled back.

"No." He shook his head.

I gaped at him, then moved into a scowl as he stepped back. Behind him, steam lifted and curled from the open door to the bathroom.

"No?" I sassed.

"No. We've done this already."

I huffed, grabbing his unzipped jeans hanging unlawfully low on his hips. One tug pulled him closer, and I secured him in a hard kiss again. He growled, taking hold of my hips as he held me in place. Dipping down, he arched me back with the force of his kiss. He could tell me no, but he was showing me the opposite.

"And you want me to believe that once was enough?" I demanded when he parted for air.

"It has to be." He stared at me with such need burning in his eyes that I feared I'd burn up under his gaze. "You can't stand me."

I shook my head and kissed him harder, dizzy under his responding touch and from his turning me toward the wall. My back smacked against the surface, and I relished his dominance as he pinned me there. We were right next to the open bathroom door. Steam curled around us, heating it up even more, as if we weren't scorching already. My skin felt too tight. My pussy ached. I was already so damned aroused by the idea of this rugged man that I couldn't stand any chance of distance between us. I wanted him in me. I wanted to be on him. I wanted us together so tight and slick, with no gap, so we couldn't tell where he ended and where I began.

"I can't stand wanting you when I know you're all wrong for me."

He nodded, groaning as I shoved his jeans lower and tugged at his boxers. "I can't stand you either." With a swift pull, he tugged my shirt up and over my head. I'd changed since we came home, and I was so happy I'd left out a bra. "Fuck. I can't stand you," he repeated as I grabbed his dick and pumped his hard length. I only got a couple of strokes up and down before he moved out of my reach. Lowering to suck and kiss my breasts, he kept his cock too far from my hands.

"You uptight, bratty diva," he growled, panting hard as he cupped my tits and pulled my bead of a nipple between his lips. "A pain in the ass."

I moaned, letting my head roll on the wall as he moved to my other breasts and tortured my sensitive flesh there with his tongue, teeth, and lips. So hungry. So demanding.

"I can't stand you, but I want you so fucking bad, Eva."

"Me too," I gasped, excited and not turned off by how he growled his complaints. "You're not right for me, but you feel so fucking good." I squirmed out of his hold, sacrificing the sweet torture of his kisses and touches on my breasts. Lower now, I took hold of his veiny, hard length and stroked him.

He groaned, humping into my hand before he kissed me again. With his hands on the wall, he rocked into my fist.

"I need you. I shouldn't want you, but I need you."

He nodded, kissing along my jaw until he aimed for my breasts again.

"You protected me."

He stopped. He froze and gripped my chin. "Are you confusing desire for gratitude? I don't want you to fuck me as payment for keeping you safe."

Oh, God. He was so fucking sexy, making me own up to *why* I wanted him.

"No." I kissed him as I swirled my thumb over his pre-cum to lubricate stroking him slower. "But seeing you rush to my safety was fucking hot." It was thrilling that he'd want to protect me when he had no obligation to. It emphasized that deep down, he *did* care.

"*You're* too hot for me to handle. I should stay away while I can." I ran my free hand up his chest, reveling in the ridges and dips of his muscles and taut abs. So strong, oozing testosterone and frying my nerves with lust.

"Fuck, Eva. You can't…" He finished whatever he could've said with a low growl as he picked me up and carried me into the bathroom. "You can't say shit like that to me."

I shoved my shorts and panties off as he fumbled with his jeans. Kissing made it harder to stand, but his muscled arms were around me before I could fall. Before I could even get my shorts and panties off, he had me in his arms and under the water. He carried me into the shower, soaking us and the clothes I hadn't removed yet.

"We shouldn't do this," he said, cringing as I pumped his erection. He lifted me, urging me to wrap my legs around his waist. "We're not right for each other."

I nodded. "We're horrible."

"We don't match," he argued between sloppy, ravenous kisses.

"We don't," I agreed, grinding against his dick and hoping he'd get inside me soon. I was about to combust, overwhelmed with desire.

"This is the last time."

He notched his cockhead at my entrance, teasing me.

"Last time," I agreed, nodding. "One more time."

His fingers curved over my ass cheeks as he slowly fed his cock into my pussy. Slower than he had in the closet, he savored the sinking thrust.

"It's just sex," he growled near my ear as he hesitated, halfway in.

I kicked my heel into his ass and tugged him to keep going. I'd cry if he tormented me any longer. I was hit with too many intense sensations to last long. My nipples ached from the abrasion of his hard chest rubbing against my breasts, shoving them higher. My clit throbbed, needing more friction. I was stretched, so full but not enough. I needed all of him, as deep as he could go.

"Just sex. It doesn't mean anything," I replied, lost to desire.

"Yeah. Nothing. This means nothing, Eva." He groaned, pushing further into me as the water slicked down our bodies.

"Nothing. Means. Nothing at all," I mumbled back. "I don't even like you."

He grunted, pulling back out and sliding all the way in again. "But I fucking can't get enough of you wrapped around my dick like this. Squeeze me, Eva. Suck me in and squeeze me."

I clung to him as he pounded into me faster. His hands remained on my ass. I tightened my legs around his hips. With the leverage of his chest pushing me against the shower stall, he had enough momentum to build and use on me.

"Oh, yeah. Like this. Just like this," I begged.

As long as he could fill me so deliciously like this, like a wild animal, grunting and rutting into me with such speed and force, nothing else could matter.

"Yeah. You like bouncing on my cock?" He kissed me, stealing my chance to respond.

I moaned into his mouth as he leaned back. Keeping my upper back on the wall, he canted back so he could stare at my tits jiggling and bouncing with the ferocity of his thrusts.

"You want this?"

I gasped, watching him watch me as he fucked me hard. "I *need* this. I need you. Just like this."

He scowled, his expression turning hotter and smoldering as he watched me move my hands to my breasts. My fingers slid over my wet flesh easily. As I cupped my breasts and lifted them in offering to him, he growled and pulled out of me.

"Fuck yeah, Eva. Fuck yeah." He kissed my breasts, sucking all the water off them and tormenting the throbbing need he'd abandoned in my pussy.

Before I could gather my wits to protest, he slid me back down the wall. All the way until I was seated on his dick again. "Fuck!" I cried out at the hard stretch, relishing the twist of pain and pleasure.

I tugged on my nipples, harder and faster. Between playing with them and taking every hard inch of him, I shattered quickly. My orgasm plowed through me, lighting me up from head to toe. It crushed me, broke me. In the most glorious ride on his dick, I felt the burn of pleasure everywhere. In my breasts that were so heavy with an achy need. Along my legs as they quivered and shook.

Then in the deep pulse of his dick jerking inside me. He growled, leaning close and trapping my hands between us. His lips found mine, and while he kissed me, I swallowed down every bit of his groan as he came hard.

We stayed plastered together, dragging out the pleasure of him fitting me so fully. Kissing and holding each other, we slowed the intensity and gradually caught our breath. His lips brushed my cheek, and I caressed his back in lazy strokes.

After the hot fury of how we'd come together, I clung to him with a gentler hold. And he didn't seem to be in any rush to release me. His thick, hard arms stayed wrapped around me, and he didn't make a move to let me go.

Even though we agreed this was the last time. That it was just sex. He only protected me because... that was who he was. Not because he cared so deeply for me.

Our attraction burned on anger and irritation, but for a quick moment, when he'd sheltered me, I got it in my head that fondness might play a factor in there.

Just sex. And that was the last time.

Maybe if I repeated it, I'd remember it long enough for it to stick.

I lowered my legs, and as I moved, he got the hint that I wanted to get down.

"Running away again?" he teased.

I smirked at him, not prepared to let him have the last word.

"It was just sex," I reminded him, hating every syllable of that phrase.

He nodded, sobering up and losing that playfulness. "Yeah. Just sex. For the last time." His hungry gaze at my wet breasts suggested he might be rethinking it.

With a gentle squeeze of my hip, he stepped closer and kissed the top of my head. Then he moved to the side, forcing his face into the water as he shoved me aside then slapped my ass.

Did you just shoo me out of here? I glowered at him and turned to leave.

Just go. If I tried to insist on anything more... He could just tell me no again and reject me to a point where I couldn't handle it. He might not be fond of me, but dammit, I was starting to slip and care too much. This curiosity was growing into something too deep.

No. It's just sex like we agreed. Go.

As I grabbed a towel and wrapped it around myself, I tried to make peace with that, feeling like a liar the whole walk out of his room and toward mine.

11

LIAM

Several days of avoiding Eva wore on me.

We'd agreed on that shower sex being the last time, but every time she stayed at the big house in her wing, or when she passed through, usually talking with Nina or Tessa, she seemed fated to pass me by.

Quick glimpses felt longer than they lasted. Every near brush or closeness seemed to draw us together, like a heavier pressure hung in the air.

Tension. It hadn't let up, and I wondered if the others in the room could tell how much we were aware of each other—despite our best attempts at trying to hide it.

It made for a lot of stress, and while it was something of our own making, no other alternative seemed likely. I couldn't keep fucking her hard and thinking it could stay casual between us. It started to seem like we were putting off the inevitable, but I was fortunate to have Olivia as an obstacle to seeking out the slim brunette who'd captured my attention.

While I was grateful for the help, which Tessa, Nina, and even Danicia offered freely, I wanted to build the bond I was forming with Olivia. She was more relaxed around me, and I was quickly applying the tricks and tips I'd learned from so many sources. Playing with her equaled a happy Liv, and the more I did, the better she slept.

Already, I caught myself envisioning a future with her, a future I never realized I could've wanted. I could see her getting bigger and walking more confidently, then running, jumping, and climbing. Maybe I was predisposing my ideas, picturing her as a tomboy who could keep up with me and enjoy the outdoors, but also, I envisioned her dancing in tutus and insisting on tea parties.

It seemed impossible to fall in love so fast, but I was. I was living proof of that magical phenomenon that I couldn't remember how I ever could've thought I was living a good life without her in it. There was before Olivia and after, and those two existences were not at all the same. This sweet little girl was rapidly encouraging me to be the best man, the best daddy, I could possibly be—and not just because she had no one else and I had to do right by her, but because she'd so quickly stolen my heart.

However, it was exhausting. Every night we went to bed, I prayed she'd sleep through it. And every morning when she babbled and woke me up, I lay silent and tired, hoping she'd fall back asleep for just five more minutes. It amazed me that such a small person could wear me out, but I wasn't ashamed to admit I was tired and needed to vent.

Stressed about this pull to Eva. Tired from handling a baby. It added up. So when my bike was delivered at the end of the week, I was glad that Dante and Nina offered to watch Liv while I went out for a ride.

Dante followed me outside, holding Olivia while Nina changed into a bathing suit. It seemed my girl was loving the water so much that I was looking into getting her lessons.

"We'll find her one," Dante said. "I was the same. As soon as Romeo saw the pool, he wanted to always swim, but I was nervous."

I arched my brow, smiling at this supposedly fearsome Mafia boss. He never pushed me to join the family. He wasn't an asshole to me. Glancing at him holding my daughter, he looked like a young grandpa, at ease and happy to help.

"You have a certified swim instructor on staff?" I asked, teasing.

"No. But we can easily find one. In fact, I could arrange for mine."

I laughed once. "I thought Nina wasn't due until the spring."

He shrugged. "Early spring, but we should start the lessons as early as we can for him or her." His smile was genuine, and I wondered how the hell he balanced it all. Killing and torturing people, arranging drug deals, and transporting guns one minute, then turning around and being the casual family guy.

I sighed, wondering how I thought I was any different. I'd killed many, but did doing so for the sake of the military really spare me any judgment?

"I also remember my bike." He smiled at the only vehicle I'd cared to keep. I had yet to get a car, but that was mainly because I could use the many vehicles here on the property.

"You? You don't strike me as a biker."

He rolled his eyes. "I wasn't a biker. I can't stand those motherfuckers."

"Mum uckers," Olivia repeated.

Dante and I widened our eyes at each other.

"Um. I guess maybe we can start watching what we say around her..."

He laughed. "You said *we*. Are you starting to see yourself staying here with us?"

I shrugged. "I'm thinking about it."

His smile was confident and easy, almost smug, like he knew he wouldn't have to pressure me. "Yes," he said, changing the subject, "I had a Harley."

"*Had?*"

He sighed and nodded. "I was out for a ride with Nina's father. That was how long ago it was. Way, way back when. Unfortunately, it made me too easy of a target. I was shot while riding it once, and it was enough to make me reconsider."

"That blows." I wasn't a biker either. I rode, but not passionately like the fact that I had a motorcycle was part of my identity. "No one should force you to give up something you enjoy."

I mentally cringed, wondering if that was what I was doing with

Eva. We enjoyed each other in a physical way, so why not take advantage while we could, right?

After kissing Liv, I told her to behave. "I'll be back soon," I said as I got on the seat. "Just a ride to clear my mind."

Dante nodded at me, gesturing for Liv to wave bye to me.

Damn, that man's smitten with her. He would be a good grandpa. And dad. I rode, laughing at the idea that he could have both at the same time. If Romeo and Tessa were expecting…

I rode through the evening, going with no destination in mind. It freed me from the woes and constant worries and questions plaguing my mind, but it didn't erase Eva. She lingered, no matter how focused I was.

I got off and stretched at a bar off the highway, realizing it'd been too long since I'd sat in that seat. After using the restroom, I ordered a beer to relax for a little longer.

Staying at the Constella mansion wasn't oppressive. There was so much room that it didn't feel like I was stuck there or a guest at a resort. Still, it was nice to break away and have an hour or so to myself.

"Hey," a fellow veteran said after I took a stool. His short sleeves revealed a tattoo showing what troop he'd served in, and I nodded as a greeting.

"You still serving?" he asked.

I raised my brows. "How'd you guess?"

He laughed, an old, raspy sound that reminded me of Ethan. This vet was probably a lifelong smoker too. "Eh, the way you stand and hold yourself, like a soldier on alert. That and the fact that you ain't grown your hair out yet."

I smiled. "I just left, about three weeks ago." Saying that out loud felt strange. So much had changed in that short time. Finding out about Olivia, getting the official news that I would never be on full active duty again.

Then coming to see Tessa and learning that she was marrying into the Mafia. And meeting Eva.

Wanting Eva. Loathing her. But mostly, just wanting her.

"How are you adjusting?" he asked, his croaky voice cracking with every word.

"It's a work in progress." I sighed and sipped my beer. "Adjusting isn't something that happens overnight."

"I know exactly what you mean. I was discharged five years ago, and for the first four and a half, I didn't know what the fuck to do with myself." He shook his head but then chuckled. "But I'm good now. Now I'm really good."

"Glad to hear it."

He coughed a bit before speaking again. "I ain't got my cut right now. My old lady's fixing it, but I swear that it was the best thing I ever done."

I furrowed my brow. "What was?"

"Joining the club."

A motorcycle club? I didn't react, but internally, I groaned. My opinion of biker gangs was the same as Dante's. The world could do without them.

"My newfound brothers helped me. They sure did. Joining up with them all gave me a better sense of fitting in, you know?"

I did know. That brotherhood and mentality of having a kinship was a big reason I was considering working for the Constellas. I spoke with Dante, Romeo, and Franco daily, and I never left a conversation mad or offended. They *were* good men from what I saw.

"It's not easy, fitting back in with society after seeing the shit we do overseas and fighting like we do. Ya know?" He nodded, narrowing his eyes with a sage expression of recollecting his past. "After the kind of combat we survive, we ain't whole and proper to fit in with common folks again."

I shrugged, not sure it was as cut and dry as he was making it out to be. I wasn't a savage after fighting in the military. But I did feel like I'd make the most of my life in some sort of demanding law enforcement field.

"You should join."

I set down my beer, mostly empty already with how thirsty I was. "Join you?"

"The MC." He nodded, sizing me up with a careful look.

I stood, uninterested in his unsolicited advice. The last thing I wanted to do was join a bunch of bikers. I had a baby to care for. A life to live. Being on the road was fine sometimes, but I recognized the need to settle. "I'm not interested," I told the old man. Another nod was the best I wanted to do for a farewell with this stranger, already feeling like I'd wasted enough time here listening to him.

I headed back outside, mulling over how much his advice to join a crew of bikers was a hard pass for me. Yet, the idea of taking Dante up on his job offer sounded better and better every day. He was right. I did see myself as part of them, being there for almost two weeks now.

But fucking Eva would be out of the question. Continuing anything with her—just sex or not—wouldn't be smart. I heard Dante the other day. He considered Eva his daughter, and I couldn't mess up a job by sleeping with the boss's daughter.

It seemed like we just couldn't help ourselves, though, and I worried that push and pull would snap between us sooner than later.

On the road again, I paid attention to the louder roar of bikers following me. They'd left the bar when I had, but passing the first intersection was the test I was waiting for. When they didn't turn but instead sped up after me, it was too damn clear that they were chasing me.

I revved my engine, increasing my speed, and they did likewise.

Fuck. What now?

I wasn't in the mood to be reckless, and I didn't want to have trouble following me all the way back to the house.

All I had on me was one gun. It was enough for an ordinary circumstance of self-defense. As I pulled over at a gas station, I counted the assholes who followed me to the lot. Six bikers didn't count as ordinary circumstances, but I braced myself for a fight.

They looked like they were spoiling for one. As one, they got off their bikes and approached. With puffed-out chests and standing as tall as they could to look down at me and seem superior, they carried an angry vibe.

Goddammit.

"Is there a problem?" I asked, not making a move to startle them.

Behind them, I noticed others stopping for gas and glancing over, worry and curiosity on their faces.

"Yeah, asshole. We got a real problem," the one with the thickest beer belly claimed, slurring his words and staggering in his step.

Great. This is just great. Drunk bikers. I sighed for patience. *Why me? Why does this have to happen to me?*

"And what's that?"

"You came trespassing on our territory," he accused.

For fuck's sake. "No, I didn't. I'm just passing through."

"I say you ain't," he growled, flashing a knife at me.

12

EVA

"**W**ould you like to hold her?" Nina asked. She raised her brows and widened her smile as I looked between her and Olivia in her lap. The sweet girl was content to chew on the tip of her bottle, gumming around it instead of just drinking her milk.

"Oh, no." I shook my head, too put on the spot to admit that I wanted to. I'd been watching her and wondering if she'd approve of my holding her. Tessa and Nina were quick to call themselves aunties, but I lacked that maternal instinct they seemed to have with ease. I was curious. I felt a yearning to cuddle her, but I never had. I lacked experience with any babies, and Olivia was already over a year old. She wasn't a newborn to get used to from the get-go. She was a smart girl, and I was nervous she'd just know I had no clue what I was doing.

Babies could be intuitive like that, right?

"No. It's okay." It wasn't okay, but I was too intimidated that I'd mess up with something new. I wasn't personable with most people, and that was adults. I'd been raised to stay powerful and aloof, to assume everyone was out to get me. It wasn't an ideal mindset to have for good, and I worried my "icy bitch" persona that Liam accused me of would come through and scare Olivia.

"Oh, damn it," Nina said with such an exaggerated flair that I knew she was faking her shock and dismay.

"Dam!" Olivia repeated, grinning around her bottle.

Nina and I glanced at each other, sharing a silent *oh, shit* look.

"I mean, oh *dang* it," Nina amended. "She spilled a drop of milk on me. I better go wash it off." She stood, not giving me a chance to protest as she handed Olivia over.

"What—wait—what—no." Nothing I said mattered. She was on her feet and slipping back from the table, a triumphant smile on her face.

"Hey, aren't you planning to breastfeed, though?" Dante asked as he wrapped up a game of cards with Romeo. "And you'll be getting milk everywhere?"

"I don't think it's like water guns." Tessa set down her cards, folding anyway. She mimicked spraying out water from her chest. "She won't be leaking it all over the place."

"Oh, hush," Nina said, not even going far to tend to any made-up milk spill. Olivia's bottle was empty, anyway. Instead, Nina stood at the counter and snacked on the chips we had set out.

We didn't do formal game nights—ever—but it was a relaxed evening of all of us in the same place for once that we figured we should do something besides hanging around the pool. Olivia cried when water splashed into her eyes earlier, and that ended that fun.

With a fire roaring under the mantel, our hot cocoa or adult drinks consumed, and a lousy game of poker completed, we'd made a decent night of this fall evening.

Too bad Liam's not here, though. I missed him more than I had any right to. But as I held his daughter and smiled back down at her gazing at me, I wanted him to see this side of me. The kinder side, the part of me that wanted a baby of my own one day.

Seeing as he was the only man to hold my interest for more than a passing glance, that was saying a lot.

"See?" Nina gestured at me. "Livy's been seeing Eva around so much that she had to be familiar with her. I wanted to test out whether she could hold her."

I frowned at her. "So, I'm an experiment?"

Nina winked. "Nah. Just wanted to corner you into holding her because you seem too shy to ask to hold her."

Guilty as charged. I wasn't shy about it. I was simply clueless how to ask or bring it up. Nina and Tessa had appointed themselves as suitable babysitters. Sure, they knew Liam for longer, but I was here all the time too since my house was being repainted.

And if I were to ask Liam himself if I could watch her, that would require me to approach him. Which went flatly against our return to carefully avoiding each other. It seemed he was stronger in the department of keeping things to *just sex* and *only one more time*.

Since he held me in the shower, I wanted him more and more. Each time intensified my need, and I wasn't sure if I'd burn for him forever, at an accumulative pace of more lust, or if this connection would fade and fizzle if we didn't feed the attraction between us. It felt like a game of limbo, not sure of where we'd end up.

"Where is Liam, anyway?" Romeo asked around a big yawn.

"He went out for a ride," Nina said.

"Argh. I hated it when he said he got a motorcycle," Tessa said. "They're so dangerous."

"Not as dangerous as supposedly trespassing on a goddamn MC's territory," Liam drawled.

We all turned, not noticing him enter the great room. He wasn't limping, but something was bothering his leg to warrant a slow, off-kilter stride like that.

"Liam!" Tessa stood and faced him, gaping at the wounds he sported.

My heart stilled as I held Olivia, clutching her closer as though she'd notice her father so hurt and be scared. "What happened?" I hoped Olivia couldn't feel my heart racing and get fussy, but I couldn't hide my reaction.

His lip was split. Red, puffy skin raised in a circle around his eye. A scrape bled on his jaw, too. That was limited to the skin that was visible to us. I feared he'd taken more hits elsewhere that we couldn't see.

"Where did you go?" Romeo said, shooting to his feet. Like the rest of us, he was alert and concerned, taking in all the injuries that bled or swelled.

"I'm calling Danicia."

Liam exhaled a long breath, showing how exhausted and beaten he was. A protest might have been on the tip of his tongue, but he wasn't so stubborn as to actually turn down medical care.

"Probably for the best." He winced as he staggered another step into the room, and Franco stood there to help him or catch him if he fell. "I rode off the highway a bit."

"To the east or the west?" Romeo demanded.

"West. I stopped at a roadside bar near Lannin."

"Fuck." Romeo glanced at Dante, who frowned after setting his phone down.

"I couldn't get Danicia, but I left her a message."

Liam huffed, waving him off. "Whatever."

This was not a situation to dismiss with a grumpy *whatever*. I stood, holding Olivia still, worried that she'd gone quiet because of how wounded Liam looked but also because of his grimace. I'd caught on quickly that babies—or at least this one—were perceptive of the facial expressions they saw on others. It made perfect sense. And unfortunately, Liam was about as approachable as a cross bear, scowling and grimacing in pain.

"That's near the Devil's Brothers' compound," Nina said with a shaky voice. She stepped closer to Dante, who grabbed her hand and held it on his shoulder.

Liam groaned. "Do I even want to know?"

"Did anyone mention any names?" Franco asked.

Liam drew in a long breath and shrugged one shoulder. "I didn't catch them referring to each other with anything but road names."

"Any stand out?" Romeo asked.

"Yeah. Bones. Oh, and Reaper."

Oh, shit. I shared a worried glance with Tessa and Nina, recognizing the President of the MC who'd teamed up with the Giovannis to take us down. The Devil's Brothers MC had already killed off and broken up the Domino Family, a rival of ours. Now that Dante had stood up to Reaper and Stefan Giovanni—more than once—he'd ensured that those two groups would be hellbent on attacking us.

"But Liam?" I wondered aloud.

"What?" he snapped, looking up at me.

While I hated his attitude, I didn't hold it against him. He'd been hurt by someone who couldn't have known was an enemy.

"I don't know," Romeo replied to me, seeming to think the same thing.

"What the hell are you saying?" Liam demanded. "Who are these fuckers?"

"The Devil's Brothers MC are led by an asshole named Reaper."

Liam shifted on his feet, favoring his right. "And let me guess, this MC isn't a fan of your family."

Franco shook his head. "No, they are not."

Liam narrowed his eyes at Nina and then at Dante. "Wait. This is the MC you stole her from?"

Nina winced but Dante glowered. "No. She never belonged to them. She shouldn't have been bet on in the first place."

"But you waded into their affairs and started this all—"

Dante stood. "No. I don't care how it looks or what it sounds like."

Liam shook his head. "Hey, I'm not saying to hand her over or anything, but that's what started it all. Right?"

"Wrong." Dante took Nina's hand and held it tight, offering her his support no matter what. Through the good times and bad, my uncle would always root for her. It was that kind of partnership and love that I worried I'd never find. A strong man to stand up for a strong woman.

"That MC was trying to stir trouble with us even before I ran into her and learned about this bet. They're a new power here, and from day one, I've been clear that they can't mess with the Constella organization. And that will always remain true."

"What I don't understand is why they'd target Liam," Romeo said. "He's not one of us."

"Not officially," Franco said.

I watched Liam as he glared at them both. He was mad, rightly so, but I worried things would be said that no one could take back.

I'd witnessed countless arguments and plenty of fights. I was no stranger to violence. Since I was a child, I've seen many men wounded —bleeding, bruised, and even missing body parts and gruesome gashes from torture. I cared about each and every man in this family, my relatives and all the soldiers and capos in the organization. Seeing Liam so hurt was harder, somehow. It pained me to know he was hurt, and through no fault of his own.

"Would you like me to help compress the bleeding?" I asked, hating how quietly and carefully I measured my words.

"No." He scowled, caught up on other details. "I *don't* work for you," he reminded Dante.

"But you've been here," Romeo said. "If anyone's been watching, they are aware that you're a guest here."

"Fuck," Tessa mumbled, shaking her head. "I never wanted to invite you to danger."

Liam scoffed, "Not like it's been much different from being in the army, Tess."

"Maybe they've spotted you here," Franco said, "or word is out that you were shopping with Eva that day and protected her."

"Son of a bitch," Dante growled. "Those fucking bikers could've been the ones to put the hit on her to attack us. To take her out. If they hired the goddamn sniper, they'd know firsthand that he protected her."

"But I *don't* work for you," Liam repeated. "This is bullshit."

"What did you do?" Romeo asked.

Liam scowled at him. "Nothing. I went for a ride and stopped at a random bar. Some old vet was talking to me about how hard it is to adjust after getting out of the military and said he enjoyed being in an MC."

"The Devil's Brothers?" Franco asked.

"No. He didn't say. I left, and a bunch of them followed me to a gas station. They claimed I was 'trespassing' and picked a fight."

"You leave any of them alive?" Dante asked.

"Yes. I only shot them to deter them from chasing after me, and I came here." He stood, slamming his fist on the table. "Where I got the association of being an enemy without even realizing it."

The sound startled Olivia, and I hugged her close, shushing her as I rubbed her back.

It didn't help. She was scared, dropping her empty bottle and breaking into a fit.

"Shit. Dammit. Liv..." Liam groaned as he walked closer, reaching out for her. "I'm sorry. I didn't mean to scare you."

I didn't keep her from him, but as he took her, she didn't immediately calm. She cried, her face turning red as he held her against him, but I didn't step back. He was steady on his feet and not falling, but I couldn't be sure he wasn't too wounded to hold her for long, much less walk with her.

He wouldn't put her at risk. If he was hurt to the point he couldn't hold her, he wouldn't push the issue. "Come on." He groaned, heading toward the other end of the room to leave us. "We can talk about this more tomorrow," he said.

I glanced back at my uncle and cousin, then Franco. No one walked off like that. No soldier would tell them how it was. But as I hurried after Liam and Olivia, Dante nodded at me, like giving me permission to follow them.

Liam wasn't a soldier. He wasn't a Constella employee, but a guest. He wasn't trying to disrespect my uncle. He was simply mad and coming to terms with all the danger we were too used to and desensitized to.

"Liam, wait."

I rushed after him all the way to the room. My heart cracked and broke with every cry little Olivia let out, but I wasn't sure I could be any better with her in this state.

"Liam."

He didn't turn or acknowledge me, striding faster to his room despite his wounded leg.

Once he pushed open the door to his guest suite, I hurried in after him before he could shut the door in my face.

"Let me—"

"No." He growled it, rubbing Olivia's back as he tried to calm her. "I don't have time for this, Eva. Time for you."

I frowned at his harsh words, damning him for not hearing me out. I wasn't here for me. For anything *I* wanted. I only wished to help *him*.

"I don't have time to scratch a fucking itch, all right?" He shook his head and paced with Olivia. "I've got a kid to take care of and calm down. I need to clean myself up after that all that bullshit with the bikers. I don't have time for anything for you."

I stepped back, hurt more than I should've allowed. He was speaking out of anger. I knew that, deep down. I was aware of the situation and what could be dictating how he behaved. But being mad was no excuse to lash out at me.

I'd taken worse insults before and not cared one bit. Yet, the way he'd worded his rejection stung.

According to him, in the heat of the moment as he reacted to my following here, I was nothing more than a body to fuck, not a person who could offer him comfort and assistance. I wasn't an expert with Olivia, but I cared, dammit. I cared about him and his daughter, enough that I'd try and do my best to support them in this tough moment of running high on emotions.

Liam didn't see me as a friend or even a close acquaintance who could offer help.

I was just someone he fucked. Only something physical.

Although I was starting to care—a lot—it seemed that he wouldn't ever be on the same page as me. I was someone to fuck. An itch to scratch.

"It's okay. I've got you. It's all right, Liv," he crooned, trying to calm his baby as he gave me his back.

I wasn't sure that I could convince myself of the same. Without a word, I turned and left him as he'd ordered.

It wasn't okay that he'd been hurt. All he truly had was Olivia, no one else. And I was certain that would never be all right in this world we'd come to share. It couldn't be *all right* when I was this hurt and maligned and being told to get lost when I was slowly opening my heart up to both of them.

I wanted to be here for him, however he needed me to make this night less of a nightmare.

But this time, it was impossible for me to fight his harsh rejection. This time, he could have the last damn word.

I knew my worth. I was aware of my value. And I'd be damned if I begged him to see me as something more than a convenient piece of ass to enjoy when he wanted company.

13

LIAM

Olivia eventually calmed down.

I couldn't say the same for myself. After I laid her in her crib, I sat in the silence of the guest room and regretted how I'd lashed out at Eva. She'd tracked me back here, wanting to see me, but I couldn't handle any sympathy or concern after what I'd gone through tonight.

I showered and cleaned up my cuts and scrapes from fighting back those bikers, but being in the shower stall and under the massaging water pressure reminded me of *our* shower we'd shared. How she came apart with me so beautifully like we were made for each other.

I was a mess, inside and out, but mostly in my head. I was livid that anyone would target me just because I'd been spending time here with the Constellas. Tessa was the only reason I'd come—to check on her and catch up—but that was no excuse for hanging around.

No reason to explain why I'd been shopping with Eva and so eager to protect her from that sniper.

If pushing her to safety marked me as one of them, if that action declared me an ally of the Constellas...

Then fuck you, Reaper. Fuck you all.

I would never hesitate to defend another, especially in something so impersonal as a distant shot from a sniper. That was cold-blooded murder. An assassination.

As I lay in my bed and tried to relax to rest, my mind ran a mile a moment with the fear that Eva could ever be killed. Or hurt. With or without me in her life.

She'd come to matter that much, regardless of how constantly I'd coach myself to push her away and keep my distance.

I cared, and I'd fucked it all up by telling her that I felt the opposite.

When I walked in and saw her holding Olivia, it hit me hard. The image of her with my child was a peaceful, safe one. One that I liked and would've taken another moment to savor if I hadn't been hurt and pissed.

Eva wasn't just someone to fuck and have fun with. We were toxic, opposites and so combative, but when we came together, it just made sense.

Realizing how much my feelings were changing was a challenge to accept. Facing that realization when I felt wounded and targeted—unjustly—had me fighting it all the more.

"Dammit," I muttered, knowing that I'd need to apologize and somehow explain that I hadn't meant a word of what I'd shouted. I didn't want to scratch an itch with her. I wanted more than a causal fuck buddy.

And that means I need to stick around and make it right.

The next morning, I headed down to breakfast, hoping that I'd see Dante. For once, he wasn't making breakfast. Tessa was.

"Hey," she greeted, quickly smiling at Olivia waving at her.

"Hi. Hi. Hi."

I couldn't help but be in a better mood. No matter how shitty I slept, hearing my daughter's little voice so peppy and happy improved my outlook on life.

"How are you doing, Liam?" she asked as I set Olivia in the high chair that I'd bought for her. It was compact and easy to stow away, not taking up much space as we overstayed as guests in this house.

"I know you're fine. You've always been so tough. But about... why that happened last night."

"Also fine." I glanced at her as I strapped Liv in. "I was hoping to see Dante."

She raised her brows. "To tell him that you want to take off?"

I shook my head. "To accept his offer."

She set her hands on the counter and tilted her head to the side. "You do?"

"Yeah. I do."

"Because of last night?"

"Because it makes sense." I rubbed the back of my neck. "What that vet said to me in the bar got to me. I slept on his unsolicited advice, and things seem clearer now. It is weird to readjust to civilian life, but I need to figure out a path forward." I gestured at Olivia. "For her."

She nodded, smiling softly. "Yeah, you do."

"You're the closest thing I have to family, Tess, and if I can find another 'family' through you..." I shrugged. "Then I'd be an idiot not to appreciate it. Fitting in with a group is a blessing in disguise. While I'd never join a bunch of idiots like those bikers, I feel like I've already been indoctrinated here, with the Constellas."

"And you won't worry about working for the 'bad guys' or anything like that?"

I smirked at her. "As if I've always been a saint."

She laughed. "No, you haven't, you smug, stubborn bastard." She winced and covered her mouth, catching herself too late for cursing around Olivia. Fortunately, she was more preoccupied with the toy on the high chair tray to care about what was said between the adults.

"If I'm going to be identified as someone within the Constella Family, then I may as well act the part," I added.

"I'm glad you'll stay." She looked down and furrowed her brow for a pensive moment. "I worry every day that Romeo could be hurt. Dante, Franco, all of the men. And now, I'll worry about you too, but I already had been doing that."

I approached her and pulled her in for a hug. "And I'll be as careful as I've always been."

She hugged me back for a long moment, then released me with a bright smile. "I think he's in his office. They've been up all night tracking the bikers and looking into how to retaliate."

Now that's something I'd love to get onboard with. The fucker who gave me this black eye would be reuniting with my fist in a bad way. As soon as I could make it happen.

I headed to Dante's office and knocked on the door.

"Come in," he called out. Even through the door I heard the fatigue in his voice.

"Morning, Liam." It was just him in here, despite Tessa implying that Romeo and Franco had been up with him all night, following up. "What can I do for you?" He looked me over, like taking inventory of the wounds I'd incurred last night. But he wouldn't make a fuss about them.

"You can hire me," I said as I stood at the ready, hands behind my back.

He reclined in his chair as he swiveled it to face me. "About time."

I cocked my head to the side. "What?"

He huffed a single bark of laughter. "It's been hard reminding myself that you're not already one of us. You've fit in since day one."

Not sure about that... Because I was fitting myself in your niece that first night I was here...

"You care about Tessa. Nina too. You're learning to take care of Olivia. Some men are just born with the innate need to serve and protect, and no matter where you are, you *are* a soldier at heart."

And Eva. But he wouldn't know about that. I nodded once. "I'd lay my life on the line for any of them."

"I can see that." He stood and extended his hand for me to shake. "And I'd be honored to recruit you. However..."

Dammit. I hadn't counted on a catch.

"Not just yet. You're still getting used to Olivia. Learning you're a father isn't something to rush."

"I'll look into finding a sitter for when I'm on the clock."

He deadpanned at me. "As if we won't have enough staff here wanting to help with her."

I smiled. "But I would like to find somewhere for us to stay. I'm sorry that we've been overstaying this long already as we visited."

"No worries there." He patted my back. "We've got a lot of work being done on our properties, but there are a few houses in the area you can take your pick from."

Assuming my salary will cover it? "I appreciate that. I'll pay you back once I start receiving pay."

He chuckled. "Pay that we haven't even discussed. You don't have to worry about a thing."

"No," I insisted. "I'll pay you back for your generosity."

Looking me dead in the eye, he smiled. "You already have. I'm already in great debt to *you*, Liam, for your instinct and willingness to protect Eva."

I sobered at the reminder. Covering her and making sure she was safe was likely the reason the Devil's Brothers had targeted me and picked a fight with me last night. But I wouldn't have changed a thing.

"I'd protect her a thousand times again," I replied, meaning every word.

He nodded and patted my back again. "I respect that, Liam, and I appreciate it. We've been going through a lot of changes in the family lately. Nina and Tessa coming into our lives. A baby on the way. Even you and Olivia fitting in with us. But Eva will always be the woman I consider my daughter. She's always mattered to me, and I will never stop fearing for her safety as we navigate the rising tensions with our enemies."

I swallowed, feeling put on the spot with his open admission of feeling vulnerable about her. This was becoming an awkward moment, like this wasn't a matter of me accepting his job offer and to work for his Mafia organization but more like it was a meet-the-parents sort of thing.

Dante had no clue how much Eva meant to me. As someone to play around with. Someone to share a quickie in the shower with. Even as more, as a woman I'd want to date and keep as my partner.

No one here knew that we were keeping up an affair in secret. And if this Mafia boss were aware…

How mad would he be?

He seemed so cool with me, not like a hard ass crime lord, but this was the woman he considered his daughter. His precious niece.

At the very least, I bet he would've wanted a heads up that Eva and I were…

I mentally cringed, hating myself all over again for what I said to her. I hadn't been thinking straight, reacting to the new and real threat of really wanting her. Committing to the army was easy. I struggled with committing to Dante's organization, but I'd gotten there. Settling and committing to one woman for more than a quick lay? Now that was the riskiest thought of all.

But for her, for Eva…

I was already in too deep to backtrack now.

"I consider myself a good judge of character, Liam," Dante said. "It comes with the job."

I laughed lightly, nodding. "I imagine it would."

"I've had a good feeling about you from the moment we met."

"That's impressive, considering I had to look clueless and bewildered that night I arrived."

"Becoming a father is never easy." He chuckled. "And I can only sympathize with how suddenly you learned about Olivia. But I had a good feeling about you from the beginning. You don't need to tell me or promise that you'll keep my family in your best interests. That you'll protect Eva no matter what. I know it. You are a loyal man through your actions and guardedness, and I'm honored that you'll fight with us and support the family."

He was accurate. I would be loyal. And if I had to personally protect Eva again, I damn well would, without hesitation.

But with matters of the heart, I wasn't so sure.

I doubted that I could resist her forever. That if she accepted my apology for how I lashed out, we'd be able to keep our hands off each other.

Now that I would be working for the Constella Family, this was a business deal keeping me here near her.

I had to be careful, more than ever. This gig wasn't something that just anyone could walk into like I had. I wouldn't take it for granted, which meant I'd need to improvise about how I could get away with sleeping with the boss's niece.

If she'll give me the time of the day again.

14

EVA

Tessa held up another end of the pink and blue streamers for me to measure. I hurried onto the stepstool too quickly and almost fell, making her laugh.

"Easy there," she teased. "I don't want to deal with ordering more streamers and ribbons if you crumple all these."

I smiled, recalling how Olivia had crawled into the box of party decorations Tessa and I had been going through at the big house. I'd been staying in my room there so long now while my place was being repainted that it was feeling more like the home I belonged in. With Nina and Tessa both there, it was easier to spend time with them.

And Olivia. That precious girl was too cute. Even when she crawled into the box and messed up the streamers and ribbons Tessa bought for Nina's baby shower we would be throwing at this downtown tea room in a couple of weeks. Tessa and I were here to practice setting up the décor, just to see if we had enough, or too much, or if we liked the theme of the space with the things we'd gotten already.

Dante suggested hiring a party planner, but Tessa wouldn't hear of it. Now that we were so busy preparing for it, I liked doing it ourselves too.

"Just store the boxes of supplies somewhere baby safe," I told her as

LEONA WHITE

we stretched our arms up and stuck the hanging lengths at equal loops.

"Yeah, I will. But Liv's too cute to be mad at."

You've got that right, I mused as we stepped back.

"Hmm. Maybe the middle dip can hang lower and the side ones can be higher," Tessa said.

"No." I took the seat where Nina would be at the head table. "If she's sitting here, any pictures with the low loops behind her at the height would make it look like she has horns coming out of her head."

After Tessa cracked up, agreeing, she adjusted the décor with me again. "And she really hasn't been devilish during her pregnancy."

"No. She hasn't." Nina was a sweet-mannered woman, though, so I wasn't shocked that the pregnancy hormones hadn't turned her into a crazed, mean mama-to-be.

"Now you, on the other hand," she teased.

I shot her a dirty look. "What about me?"

"You're already a handful as a pampered princess, so you'd only ramp that up if you were expecting."

I pressed my lips together and sighed. There it was again, that difficult label. It followed me through my childhood, into adolescence, and it dogged after me into adulthood.

"I'm just teasing…" She elbowed me as we searched through the boxes for more décor items to stage and place.

"I know." I was aware that she was teasing me, but it was getting old.

"Honestly, I don't know how you managed to be as normal as you are." She shook her head, musing. "Living with constant danger puts a different spin on a childhood."

"It's not so much that as the never-ending demand to be on. To look powerful. To stay aloof because everyone will want to tear you apart."

Tessa frowned at me, sad and sympathetic. "You matured too soon, huh?"

I nodded. "It can look glamorous, living in the mansion, having all your needs and desires met, the staff and guards to cater to you and keep you safe."

"But..." she guessed.

"But the power and influence can confine you too."

"Eh, Nina and I will keep you well-rounded," she joked, bumping her side to mine.

"And besides," I joked right back, "you're more likely to have a kid than me."

"Why do you say that?" She grinned, giving me a look like she had a secret on me.

There's no way she can know Liam and I have been hooking up...

"Well, there's the obvious fact that you're engaged to Romeo and busy with him, whereas I'm single."

She shrugged. "I want to wait, though."

"Yeah?" This sort of girl talk—chatting about babies—wasn't something I often did. Then again, I seldom had women I could consider close friends. Nina and Tessa were introducing me to a world of sisterhood I'd been missing out on for far too long.

"I want kids. He does too, but I'm too busy enjoying myself with him to rush it."

I scrunched my face. "Please, no more details." Romeo was more like a brother to me than a cousin. Thinking about my cousin's sex life wasn't appealing, either.

She giggled. "Okay. Okay."

"Did you always know you wanted to have children one day?"

"Yes and no. I mean, until I met Romeo, I was firmly against it. My parents were so stubborn about my marrying Elliot Hines, and I wanted nothing to do with him. They shoved that idea down my throat so much that I dreaded it coming true, and I did not want kids in the mix with someone pervy like him."

"I understand."

"What about you? I bet you're not crazy about the idea of having kids, either."

I frowned, disliking how much it hurt to be projected as a woman lacking maternal desires.

"I only say that with the way you were raised. In the Mafia. I bet you've been dreading being arranged to someone, right? There are so many levels of politics and rules I'm not aware of, but I'm guessing you can't just meet someone and choose them."

"Dante would never force me to marry someone I didn't love."

She smiled. "I know, but you can't blame me for assuming that. It is the way of other Mafia families, isn't it?"

"It is."

"So, assuming you could pick your man, would you want kids?"

I nodded, biting my lip with how risqué it felt to admit that. "I never thought I would, partly because of what you're saying about raising them in the Mafia. Who would want to bring up a child among danger?"

"Uh-huh."

"But the idea of being a mother is growing on me."

A lot. Most of this urge was due to Olivia. Having a baby in the house opened my eyes to something I wasn't used to. Nina's being pregnant added to it as well.

"Or do you mean the idea of Liam giving you a baby is growing on you?"

I gawked at her, not joining in her laughter after that blunt tease.

Does she know? I blinked quickly, stunned speechless. I didn't know if I could lie and hide that she was right or—

"I saw you sneaking out of his room. In nothing but a towel." She clamped her lips shut, as though she battled giggles. "I know."

I swallowed and held my hand over my neck. "Um…" My cheeks betrayed me, heating up with a furious blush. The tips of my ears turned hot, and I looked everywhere but at her.

"Holy shit. You're blushing!"

I furrowed my brow and cleared my throat. "Does anyone else know?"

"I didn't say a word. I wanted to ask you about it."

"To ask me about sneaking out of his room in a towel?"

She laughed, so light and easy to talk with. I knew she wasn't laughing at me, and that made a difference. "No. It's your business what you do with him, so long as you don't break his heart or anything like that."

I nodded. How can I break his heart if he doesn't even want to give it to me?

"How serious is it?" She leaned in to whisper. "Serious enough that you'll be the next one expecting?"

I shook my head. "No. Not at all." Even though Liam and I hadn't used protection, it wasn't likely to happen again. "Just a fling."

"Oh." She frowned, seeming disappointed. "I shouldn't be surprised. He's never been the kind of guy to commit for long. But I was hoping…"

I waved her off. "No, it's definitely not serious between us." God, how I wished it were, though. Liam was growing on me, but it was a one-sided effect here.

"But it's true. He is kickstarting my biological clock in a big, bad way."

"Ew…" It was her turn to scrunch her face. "Liam's like my brother. I don't want the details."

I smiled. "Something about seeing a rugged, tough military man with a sweet little baby girl… He's doing something to me, all right."

"And Liv's just so—"

Franco ran into the room, cutting her off and alarming me. I'd seen that tense expression of concern on his face too many times not to know something was wrong.

"You need to come back to the house," he ordered, rushing in while more Constella guards tracked in after him.

A sudden need for more protection could only mean danger was afoot. I scanned the tea party room we were pretending to decorate, wondering if someone was close to attacking us here. Oddly, I felt scared. For the first time, true terror filled me and I knew it was because Liam wasn't here with me. I felt safest with him.

"Let's go," I told Tessa, not needing to be ordered twice.

"But what's going on?" she protested. "We need to box all this up and store it for later and—"

"Someone will handle it," Franco replied. "We need you both to head to the house for security concerns."

"Has there been an attack? Has something happened?" Tessa said as I took her hand and pulled her to follow me out with the men.

"Reports of fighting at the gambling halls," Franco said, ushering us to the exit.

"The Hound and Tea?" Tessa guessed, referencing her old workplace where she waitressed at the steakhouse on the first floor of the building.

"Yes."

I winced, uneasy with this news. Suddenly being asked to go to safety wasn't something new. I'd experienced these out-of-the-blue calls for alarm when enemies attacked.

But at the Hound and Tea building? That was where Dante had taken Liam today, to show him around before he officially began as a Constella recruit.

Please, please be safe. Even if he wouldn't reciprocate the feelings I couldn't turn off for him, I had to hope he would be unharmed.

15

LIAM

I shushed Liv, offering her another cool teether from the fridge.

At this rate, Dante would boot us out of the house for a moment of quiet.

"Teething is the *worst*," Danicia said as she grabbed another ice pack for a soldier she was helping next door. She shook her head, pouting at my daughter fussing and crying in my arms.

"Nothing helps."

She huffed a weak laugh at my reply. "Sometimes, nothing will. Until she's done cutting through her gums..." She shrugged.

"Is everything okay?" I asked as I struggled with Olivia. I emphasized my question with a glance at the ice packs in her hands.

"Yeah. Yeah, it'll be cool. Franco brought a guard back home after he was hit."

I raised my brows. "Hit?" I didn't tell Dante that I'd work for him expecting an easy job free of dangers. I knew threats were out there, but they'd never come close to home.

"Attacks at the gambling rooms." She nodded at my phone that buzzed on the counter. "You should've gotten the message to stay in by now."

I frowned, picking up the device I hadn't been paying much attention to. Olivia wailed louder, proving the point that I was distracted. "Oh, thanks for the heads up." I didn't have any plans but to calm Liv down—if it were even possible.

As she headed off to help the guards who were brought next door, I winced at Liv's cries and skimmed over the text Franco had sent to the group thread of everyone currently staying at the house.

Franco: *Attacks at the H&T. Stay in the house until further notice.*

I supposed it was a lockdown alarm, and I'd abide by it. But I wasn't a fan of hiding. I preferred to be a man of action, on the frontline and doing all I could to ensure everyone around me was safe.

I hadn't started yet, though. Dante wanted me to wait at least a week to settle in further.

As I headed up the stairs, I crossed paths with Eva. She'd been busy since I yelled at her, and now that we would both be expected to stay inside for the night, I had no opportunity to avoid her.

"Hey," I said as she hurried along the hall.

"Is she okay?" Her eyes were open wide with concern as she looked at Olivia in my arms.

"Yeah." I blew out a big breath at my door. "Teething. She's just fussy and no matter what I do, she's unhappy."

"Oh." She pressed her hand to her chest and sighed in relief. "With the lockdown alert, I got nervous."

I tipped my head toward my room, indicating for her to follow me. "Why would you be nervous?"

"Well, if something happened or something scared her."

I knew she cared about Liv. I saw it in her eyes when she smiled at her and watched her.

"But wouldn't you have faith in the guards patrolling the property?"

She furrowed her brow, a telltale sign of her getting ready to argue with me and butt heads. "Yes. Of course, I trust them. But shit happens. Life happens."

I nodded. "Yeah. You're right."

"Like your incident with MC men at the bar." She looked away and frowned. "That stuff happens."

Olivia leaned toward her, catching her attention, and I handed her over. It didn't hurt that she wanted someone else. With the nonstop fussiness, I would take any break that I could get.

"And shit happens like me yelling at you," I said, appreciating Eva's willingness to hold Olivia and cuddle her close.

She shot her gaze to me, intrigued but on edge with what I said. "You chose to yell at me. Don't make excuses."

I shook my head. I wouldn't, but it used it as an ice breaker to bring it up. "I did, and I'm sorry that I yelled at you."

"Just that you yelled?" she asked, rubbing Liv's back. "Not what you yelled at me for?"

"All of it. I had no right to raise my voice at you like that."

She smirked. "Really? You gave yourself the right to call me a slut and a brat. A diva, too."

I rubbed my lips, fighting a smile. She wasn't tossing that back at me as an insult, but more like a sarcastic reminder. "I think it's safe to say that was different."

She shrugged, seeming to agree without saying so.

"That was dirty talk."

"Uh-huh."

"But I was wrong to yell at you when you followed me after I was attacked."

"I..." She exhaled a long breath, gazing at Olivia as she started to calm down. Her little hands gripped Eva's shirt as she clung to her, seeming to want a woman's touch, not mine. "I understand. It was a tense moment."

"It's still not okay. And I'm sorry."

"Thanks." She cleared her throat. "I only followed you because Olivia seemed so scared and worked up."

I grunted a rough laugh. "Probably because I looked pissed and scary." I pointed at my black eye.

"Yeah. I wanted to help you with her while you cleaned up and took care of yourself." Her shrug was delicate, like she wanted to act like it was nothing.

I saw her uncharacteristic action as a sign of nervousness. Was she actually intimidated by *me*? Or because of how she was feeling about me?

"She sure seems to approve of your holding her," I commented, watching how natural she was with her. Holding her close, rubbing her back, and even resting her cheek on the top of Liv's golden curls.

"I'm glad." Her smile was soft and tender, and it hit me hard.

Seeing her holding my daughter messed me up. I enjoyed the closeness they were sharing, this relationship that seemed to come out of nowhere. Eva wasn't the first woman I'd think of as being motherly, but that was only because she kept herself so guarded from everyone else.

Of course she was nurturing. I saw the evidence of it as she swayed and comforted my baby.

And it was an addictive sight to behold. Like... mother and daughter.

The image of Eva pregnant with a child—*our* child—hit me so swiftly, I couldn't resist it. I didn't try to. Instead, I welcomed the immediate daydream, suddenly obsessed with making it happen.

Of seeing her as my partner.

My wife.

The mother of my kids, so loving and generous like she was with Olivia right now.

"Fuck it," I muttered to myself.

I didn't want to hold back on the allure of the fantasy. She was right here, gorgeous and stunning within my reach. I got lost in the trusting depths of her caramel gaze as she looked up at me with such vulnerability, such desire. As if she were thinking the same thing. As if she were hanging on by a thread in wanting me just as badly.

One step closer brought me to her. And another one put me right in her space.

She turned, protecting Olivia from my crushing into her as we stood so close together. But she didn't dodge me or attempt to hide.

That sass was clear in her eyes as she defiantly lifted her chin ever so slightly.

I caught it between my thumb and finger and tilted her face up to mine so I could kiss her until she moaned in response, setting my blood on fire with raging need.

16

EVA

No. I gasped against Liam's hot mouth as he deepened the kiss.

No. It's not supposed to feel this good.

He slid his fingers further back, cupping my face to hold me close. The taunting grip of his hand like this was an ultimate thrill. To feel like I was his to command. His to have.

No. Not like this.

I wrenched back, breathing hard as I stared at him. When I licked my lips, he tracked the moment and growled with need.

"Last time, you told me to get out." I swallowed, struggling past this urgency to shut up, go for what I really wanted, and kiss him again. "That I was just someone to fuck. A convenient piece of ass, remember?"

He furrowed his brow, and I dared him to scowl at me and deny it. I'd spent too many hours licking my wounds from his harsh words.

"An itch to scratch." I heaved in a deep breath, tormenting myself with another dose of his scent.

He smoothed his thumb over my cheek, frowning deeper.

"We said it was the last time for that *last* time." Staring him in the eyes, I stayed as bold as I could. "I want you, Liam. I won't lie. I want you so bad, but I will never let a man toy with me like that. You can't decide the terms of our attraction."

He grunted, stepping closer to wrap his free arm around me, hugging me—and Olivia—closer. It was domestic, somehow, like we were a little family of three.

"I'm sorry for what I said before."

I closed my eyes as he lowered his face to mine and brushed his lips over mine slowly.

"And I won't lie, either. It's getting harder to convince myself that we should keep this no-strings-attached." He weakened me even more with a longer, harder kiss with tongue.

"Because fuck me, Eva. Seeing you holding my daughter..." He slid his hand lower, caressing my ass and using his big hand there to push me toward him. "It's messing me up."

I smiled, slow and sly, as I welcomed his embrace. "Yeah?"

"You look good like this." He brushed my hair back, and we kissed until I grew desperate for air. "I like seeing you with her, acting like a mother might."

Like... the mother of your children? I wanted it. I wanted it so bad. Though it was sudden, it was potent and true.

I swayed, leaning against him. His deep, low tone was turning me on more, drugging me with the illusion of his wanting to commit.

"You're making me wonder if we quit screwing around in secret and fighting each other..."

I whimpered, needy and impatient, as I pulled him close for a kiss.

"If we gave up fighting, if we could—"

"Liam—oh!" Tessa's voice came and went as she burst in. She popped in and closed the door quickly, catching us so close together.

"Goddammit," Liam growled softly, stepping away.

I exhaled, feeling on edge and so riled up. She'd interrupted us, and I missed the moment we'd been sharing. Liam was so hot and cold—but so was I. Both of us lasting that long without being mean was a new record.

"What, Tess?" he demanded as he opened the door and found her wincing on the other side.

"Sorry. Really." She leaned past him to cringe at me. "So, *so* sorry. But Romeo texted me and asked that I make sure you both stay in."

"We got the message," I told her.

"Yeah, but—"

My phone rang, and after I pulled it from my back pocket and answered on speaker, I let them listen in to whatever Franco had to update us with.

"Eva? Make sure you all stay in. More guards are coming as backup just in case."

"What happened?" I asked, used to this yet not. It'd been a while since Dante would've put the order in for this much security.

"The Giovannis are attacking multiple locations. Reports of the MC are in too."

I shook my head, pissed that both of our enemies were ganging up on us. Catching Liam's scowl, I knew he was just as frustrated—no doubt on a personal level since they'd hurt him last.

"Stay in and stay alert. Ask Liam—"

"I'm here," he replied to Franco.

"Liam, stay on guard. I know you haven't officially started on payroll, but—"

"Of course," Liam answered. "I'm always on guard."

The steely glint in his eyes was no joke. He was already in protective mode, just from the word of security concerns.

"I'll call when we know more."

I disconnected the call. Liam sighed and ran his hand over Olivia's hair, watching her get sleepier as she rested against me. Her tiny fingers clutched and released on my shirt, and the little gesture melted my heart.

"So, yeah. *That*"—Tessa pointed her fingers at the phone in my hand, smiling sheepishly—"that was why I was rushing through the house to find you. Nina's staying in my room with me, nervous."

"Should I come and help—"

"No!" Tessa backed up, holding her hands in the air as she

retreated toward the door. "No, no, no. You two can carry on and... yeah. Sorry again." She hurried to turn and leave, clumsy with her rush and almost tripping into the hallway.

Once the door closed, I glanced at Liam. The moment was gone. That spell of desire was broken and a sober seriousness took over the room.

He sighed and took my hand, leading me toward the couch in the living area of his suite. "What is all of this about the Giovannis?" We sat, and he ran his hand through his hair as he sank against the cushions. "I've met some of the MC men, but what's with this other group?"

Nothing could stop me from confiding in him. He would soon be working for my uncle, and I bet he was already getting lots of information from Uncle Dante himself and Franco. I saw Liam and Franco speaking quite a bit, and I knew they'd be excited for him to officially start as a recruit. His military career was simply that impressive.

Liam fit in with us, though, regardless of his employment status. He already seemed to be one of us, and I had no qualms about speaking up.

"Stefan Giovanni, the head of the Giovanni Family, used to be one of Uncle Dante's close friends. He, Stefan, and Henry Bardot—Nina's father—used to be good buddies back in the day. Back before they all drifted apart."

He frowned. "Didn't Nina's father go into the military?"

"He did. Before he enlisted, those three were close friends. Uncle Dante took the Constella name to accumulate great power and wealth. Stefan tried to as well, but over the years, he made lousy decisions and lost a lot. He sided with the Domino Family, another rival, but the Devil's Brothers wiped them out. They fought over business, and the bikers ended them."

"Damn."

"Yeah." I sighed, relaxing with Olivia's weight against my chest. She sure looked comfy, so much so that I tried not to move with her this close to falling asleep. "When the Dominos were taken out, Stefan lost a lot of money. He lost manpower, he lost product, but most of all, he lost a ton of money in backing the Dominos against the MC. Stefan wanted to get Dante's backing, to claim the Constellas as an ally, but Dante wanted nothing to do with the Giovannis."

"Or the MC, right? Since he took Nina from Reaper?"

I winced. "Try not to word it like that."

He furrowed his brow. "What do you mean?"

"That Reaper ever had Nina to begin with. He didn't. The night Nina's brother lost that bet was the first time she ever saw the man. He never *had* her, and Dante hates the idea that he ever could've had her."

He nodded slowly. "Noted."

"Stefan has joined with Reaper, though, in retaliation to the Constellas' actions."

"Like not giving Nina up?" he guessed.

"That and the way Dante told Stefan to fuck off when he wanted our backing with gun routes. And Romeo, uh, Romeo got a little ahead of himself and pissed off the MC even more when he killed one of their lawyers."

He narrowed his eyes. "Why?"

"Because that lawyer was supposed to marry Tessa."

"Damn."

I nodded, hoping all of this wouldn't intimidate him. "If anyone were to want my opinion—"

"I do." His tone wasn't mocking, and I appreciated that.

I smiled. "Thanks. In my opinion, Dante is hoping they'll piss each other off to the point that they'll kill each other off. We can't take on both groups at once, but neither of them has staying power to remain a valid threat for long. The bikers, especially. They're new to wanting power and likely won't last. The presidents change over quickly."

"Lots of infighting," he guessed.

He sounded distant, like he was just saying something because it was his turn to speak.

I glanced up from gazing at Olivia sleeping on my chest. He was watching me with something soft yet potent stirring in his eyes.

Adoration and desire. The gentle smile tugging at his lips was sexy as hell, and at once, my libido was kicked into overdrive.

"What?" I asked quietly. "What are you looking at?"

"You." He gave in to a slow smile, a full one that tugged at my heartstrings. He was always so guarded—like I was—and it felt like a rare treat to see him at ease with me.

"You really calmed her down."

I nodded, quite proud of myself. "I'm not sure how. I don't exactly have experience with babies." As I stroked her soft hair and relished the steady rhythm of her sleepy exhales, I swore I fell in love that much more. "But I'm wondering if it's just something that clicks."

"Maybe." He reached over to rub her back, staring at her with the same feeling of gratitude, like he couldn't believe he'd been so blessed. I was so glad that this little girl had reached out to me, that she saw my face and knew she could count on me.

"I still struggle with the newness of it all. That *I'm* her dad. That I'm a father at all. I feel so damn clueless, but I'm figuring it out. She's figuring me out." He glanced up at me. "Like you are with her too."

And what about me and you? I swallowed down the urge to ask him that, but when he looked back up at me a moment later, I was convinced that he was wondering the same thing.

He gave me an apology and I accepted it.

I told him not to play games with me, and he started to suggest that we stop playing altogether and get serious.

But how? In what capacity?

What's next?

In this cozy, comfortable moment we were sharing, I felt like I was ready for anything more that he wanted to give me.

If I could be honest, I'd admit that the idea of having it all with him sounded like heaven.

But I'd be damned if I'd beg for it.

17

LIAM

She wasn't doing anything but holding Olivia, but it changed my entire perspective of her.

Gone was the icy woman from the party who looked down on me for being so different and undressed, clearly not from the upper crusts of society.

Gone, too, was the woman lusting after me and game for naughty talk and getting aroused when I called her a bratty slut in the closet.

With Liv sleeping peacefully on her chest, she looked serene and confident in a new way. Like she could adjust to life's curveballs with me and make everything look effortless. Her determination to succeed and overcome any odds was sexy as hell. A smart woman was the ultimate turn on. A brave woman to take on a fussy baby and get her to relax was somehow my kryptonite.

My phone rang, jarring me from this reflective moment of admiring her like this.

Eva jumped a bit too, but she caught herself from moving too much and waking Liv.

I grabbed the device from the table and scanned the message that had come in. "Franco," I told her. "He says the situation is under control. Both Giovannis and Devil's Brothers have been captured."

Her breath of relief mirrored the one I exhaled.

"It still wouldn't hurt to stay inside for the night," she said.

In here? With me? I nodded. "Probably wise."

She locked her gaze on me again, and I felt every bit of the pressure that hung over us. The palpable sexual tension that I didn't want to avoid anymore.

"Would it be wise for me to stay?" she asked, unafraid to speak up but delicate with her tone. Not bossy, not demanding. Simply inquisitive.

"I think it's becoming foolish to pretend this connection between us is going to fade away," I admitted.

"I never thought I'd be in this position," she replied.

"What position?"

"Of wanting you so bad but knowing it can't work." She stood, seeming too anxious to sit there so close.

"What if we can make it work?" I rose and gestured between us. "You and me?"

"As...?"

"Partners." I gently eased Olivia out of her arms to carry her to the crib. She didn't wake, and once I slowly and carefully stepped back toward Eva, I turned and took her hands. "As lovers."

She leaned in and kissed me, weakening under this pull that drew us together.

I framed her face, pouring my heart into the sweetness of pressing my lips against hers, relishing her sweet, minty taste and the hint of the wine she might have had earlier.

"It might have started as just sex," I told her as I guided her toward the bed. "But that's far less than what I want with you now." Keeping my voice low, whispering as I moved her further from the crib, I relished the promise of a challenge in her eyes.

"Oh, yeah?" she taunted, whispering as well. "And what do you want?"

I tugged my shirt off, then pulled on hers. As she lifted her arms over her head to allow me to peel the garment off, I grinned before kissing her. She wasn't wearing a bra, probably having changed into loungewear when she came home earlier. I lowered my hands to cup her heavy breasts, weighing their plumpness and groaning lowly at the warm, soft globes filling my grip.

"I want you." It was the simple truth, and I intended to have her.

She sighed as I kissed down her neck, tasting her sweet flesh and feeling her rapid pulse.

"Think you can be quiet?" I teased.

Her hair brushed against my cheek as she nodded, and I wondered if she really could be noiseless with what I wanted to do. I pushed at her shorts, sliding them over her curvy hips. Her succulent flesh broke out in goosebumps as I urged her panties down too. With every inch of her smooth skin that was bared, my dick grew harder. Stiffer. And raging to plunge into her.

I winced at the pleasurable sting of pain as she twisted her fingers in my hair, keeping me close. Every touch turned me on. Each deep exhale she released taunted me to earn more of those sexy sounds. I was hers, beholden to making her gasp and shiver with pleasure.

After a push back, I got her onto the bed. She landed with a bounce, sending those glorious tits jiggling and teasing me to capture them with my lips. Her gaze stayed on me, full of hope and trust and desire so dark and addicting that I never want to lose this memory.

Spreading her legs out, she beckoned me to her pussy. I stared at her folds, glistening pink with the cream that leaked from her.

"Don't make me wait, Liam. Please."

I smiled, swiping my finger along her wet entrance. Then I brought it to my lips in a universal gesture of silence. Her chest lifted, thrusting her breasts higher with that deep breath. Needy and impatient, she bit her lip, watching me dip my finger into my mouth and suck it clean.

"Quiet." I dropped to my knees.

The musky scent of her cream thrilled me, taunting me to taste more than that sample on my finger. Keeping my eyes on hers as I brought my face to her pussy, I stretched my tongue out to collect her juices. A long, lazy swipe from her hole to her clit had her squirming on the bed.

I reached up to grab her hands and pushed them behind her. Her fingers curled within mine, fisting the sheets she sat on. Once I hoped she understood that I wanted her to keep her hands right there, I slid mine under her thighs until her legs hung over my forearms.

Over and over, I stroked my tongue over her sopping wet entrance. Nips made her push her hips into my face. Harder sucks on her clit had her dropping her head back and fighting a moan of pleasure. I didn't slow once. I didn't delay. Sucking and licking, I kept her poised on the edge of coming.

"Liam," she whined as I played with her clit, flicking the tip of my tongue at her bud.

I pistoned my fingers faster into her slippery cunt and sucked harder on her clit.

She whined, a gasping sound that would've been a loud cry if she hadn't been holding back.

Her eyes opened wider at the sound of Olivia shifting on the crib. But fortunately, she didn't wake.

I stayed still, waiting for the silence. Save for Eva's panted breaths, it was quiet. I narrowed my eyes and dared her to be noisy again. She seemed to see the warning in my gaze because she shook her head, indicating that she wouldn't wake her.

"Want me to keep going?" I whispered before kissing her entrance and dipping my tongue in.

She nodded, moving her shaky fingers to my head. Once she threaded them through my hair, scraping her nails against my scalp, I let her guide me back down.

Worrying that she wouldn't actually be quiet, I angled up and pushed her to lie back. Reaching up to cover her mouth, I let her fuck my face as I licked and sucked.

My chin was covered with her juices, and I didn't care how messy she made us. The sluicing sounds weren't too loud to wake Olivia, but they spurred her on to reach her orgasm faster. As she came, squirting on my tongue and treating me to more of her sweet cream, I funneled two of my fingers into her mouth to keep her from being too loud.

She sucked them in hard, moaning quietly. I felt the vibration of her hum of approval, and I smiled as I licked the last of her juices as she came, shivering, trembling, and gasping. She was a puddle of pleasure, lax and limp on the bed. But I wasn't done.

"Shh," I reminded her as I pulled my fingers out and leaned up.

She blinked up at me, drowsy and sated, but still with interest burning in her eyes as I tore off my jeans and boxers, revealing my dick as it sprang up and pointed at her.

I kicked my clothes aside and stroked myself a couple of times, letting her look her fill. We'd never slowed down. We'd never attempted to have sex horizontally, and I wanted her to have a chance to see what I had for her.

She lifted her arms, beckoning me to lower over her. I did, hovering and bracing my weight on my forearms. Instead of lying still and making me do all the work, she kissed me and tasted herself. Her hands slipped over my back as she dragged her nails down my muscles. Then she rubbed over my ass and squeezed before reaching for my dick. Shifting up, she lined her pussy to my cockhead and widened her legs. Rubbing my erection over her, she guided me in.

And I was home. I slid in all the way until I was seated. Letting my hips grind against hers, I pushed her down on the mattress until she had no room to move.

"Oh..." She moaned quietly on a sexy sigh, but I feared it would be too much noise. Now that I was inside her, I wouldn't be able to give up this chance to rock her world.

I kissed her, hard but not brutally, as I thrust into her over and over again.

I wouldn't last long. Not with the pleasure of eating her cunt. Not with how tight she squeezed me, launching me closer to losing control.

When I did, we came together. Her slick inner muscles gloved me, milking me until I shot my cum deep inside her. I cradled the back of her head as she rode through her climax, clenching me until I was spent.

Finally, when I was certain that we wouldn't make noise, I broke the long, wet kiss we'd muffled our reactions with. I pressed my lips to hers once more, just because I couldn't resist. Then I reared back and smiled at the sluggish smirk of satisfaction she gave me.

"Imagine that. We made it to a bed for once."

"Da-Da."

We widened our eyes at each other, locked in a freezing paralysis of shock at Olivia's little voice. In unison, we turned to face the crib. Throw pillows formed a wall at the end of the bed to block her from seeing us, but just barely.

"Oh, my God," I whispered as a smile took over my face.

Eva nudged at my chest. "Liam! Do you think she saw us? Heard us?"

I faced her again after realizing Olivia didn't have much of a vantage point. Even if she had, she wouldn't have seen much or understood what was happening.

I couldn't wipe this stupid smile off my face. "That's the first time she's called me that." Liv knew quite a few words. Danicia assured me she was on par with her milestones, but I'd been waiting for her to call me *Daddy*.

Now that she had, I felt better. No. I felt great. My daughter recognized me. My woman was letting me love on her.

Nothing could go wrong as far as I was concerned.

I kissed Eva quickly, knowing things could only look up from this moment forward.

18

EVA

"So, you and Liam, huh?" Nina teased as we headed to the tea party room once more.

I wasn't sure if it'd taken Tessa a week to tell Nina that she'd walked in on me and Liam during a heated moment or if it had taken all this time for both women to get me in place to talk about it. We seemed to be going in different directions even though we were all in the same house, but it was only now, a week after Liam and I actually made love on a bed, that we could have our girl talk.

I wasn't one to kiss and tell, but it seemed that would be changing. We were here to discuss the catering for the baby shower, and during the wait, they seemed to assume we had much to chat about other than party preparations.

"Yep." I nodded, glancing up from the contract the venue had given us. "Didn't we invite forty guests? This only says thirty."

Nina pushed the paper down. "It can wait for a moment. Really? You and Liam?" She smiled wide, but I didn't miss the mischief in her eyes.

"Okay." I set the paper down and crossed my arms. Leaning back in my chair, I sighed and tried to be as diplomatic as possible. "You know I've never done this before."

Tessa choked on her tea. "You are *not* telling me that you were a virgin before you met him."

I furrowed my brow. "What are you implying?" I wasn't. I lost my virginity when I was eighteen with a soldier. He was unfortunately killed in a turf war a month afterward, and I liked to think that we'd at least seen to his not dying a virgin.

"Nothing." Nina elbowed her hard. "Or she shouldn't be. Your virginal status—or lack thereof—is your business and no one else's."

"Sorry." Tessa rubbed her arm where Nina jabbed her. "I'm just surprised."

It was a moot point to argue about whether I lost my virginity to Liam. But I was curious. "How so?"

"You're so…" Tessa shaped her hands in the air, gesturing at me. "So sexy. And gorgeous. Confident and cool."

Nina shrugged. "You act and look like you could chew up a man and spit him out when you're done with him."

"But have you actually seen me with any men since you've come into the family's protection?"

They shook their heads. "No," Tessa said.

"Then why couldn't I have been a virgin?" I asked.

"Well…" She winced. "I don't know. You looked too confident and intelligent to be ignorant about sex."

"I'm sure there are plenty of virgins who are educated about sex but lack experience." I held up my hand. "And I wasn't before you saw me in Liam's room last Monday."

Nina tilted her head to the side as she narrowed her eyes. "Wait. Why'd you pinpoint that day?"

"It was when I walked into his room," Tessa answered.

Nina was quick, though. She opened her eyes wide and gawked at me. "Was that the first time?"

I sighed. "I thought I just established that Liam didn't take my virginity."

"No. First time with him," she asked, high on the scandal.

"What?" Tessa dropped her jaw too. "How am I so oblivious?"

"Because you're too busy with Romeo," I muttered. Looking at them both, one at a time, I sighed again. "Liam and I... had a moment at the engagement party."

Tessa's eyes bugged out. "What? *Where?*"

"A closet." I pressed my lips together not to smile as they laughed.

"And I saw you running out of his room in a towel a couple of weeks ago," Tessa added. "But I figured you had gone swimming or something and..."

I deadpanned at her, as if to say *really?*

"Wow." Nina beamed. "You're sneaky."

Tessa grunted. "Liam was always sneaky and stealthy. It's part of why Romeo and Franco were so eager to have him join the Constella forces."

Which began tonight. I was nervous about it, yet not. Liam was, like his old friends could attest to, a smart man in the field. His protective and survival instincts were no joke. However, the idea of his willingly entering a dangerous situation tested my patience and sanity.

I didn't want him hurt. Ever.

"How serious is it?" Tessa asked, then shook her head as if regretting what she said. "Sorry. I'm so pushy."

"Nosy, more like," Nina teased.

Tessa shot her a dirty look. "Oh, like you're not excited and want to pry for info too?"

"I am. I'm just letting you do all the hard work of blurting out everything that comes to your mind."

"I don't know," I said, cutting off their sisterly and friendly bickering. "We started out as just... Well, we didn't intend to start anything. It just happened."

Tessa smirked. "You just saw him and bam?"

Nina rolled her eyes.

"Sort of. We butted heads from the get-go."

Both women nodded, as though they expected that.

"And he just..." I shrugged one shoulder. "Well, he was fine as hell before I knew he had a baby. But seeing him with Olivia..." I fanned myself.

"That biological clock started ticking," Nina guessed. "Big time."

"And in overtime," I added.

Tessa smiled, almost like she was proud to hear this. "Well, good. I think this is awesome. He's needed a woman who can put up with him, and you'll be the one to tame him."

"He's a man, not a wild animal," Nina quipped.

I picked up my teacup, dainty as I arched my brows and brought it to my lips. "Oh, I wouldn't say that..."

We dissolved into laughter, and I realized as my stomach hurt from cracking up that I was enjoying this. This foreign, new sisterhood. It wasn't intimidating. And it helped that they could add in more bawdy jokes. We *were* ladies. We looked like the polished Mafia girlfriends and fiancées we were supposed to be. But at the same time, it felt good to let loose and just have fun with them.

"Is he going to move into your house?" Nina asked. "I can't imagine it's easy to have an active sex life with Olivia in his suite."

"We haven't thought that far ahead." It sounded like a copout of a reply, but it wasn't. "We're too busy stealing every minute we can. I've been busy helping Danicia arranging some of the care for the men wounded from the latest attacks, and he's been preparing to start working for us..." I shrugged. "But we will need more space."

For a hot moment, I feared that it would be tricky to designate the lines between employee Liam and boyfriend Liam. He was a Constella soldier now, so that tied him here. But how much of a tie was I? What would matter more—his job or me?

"Oh, my God..." Nina raised her brows as she spotted someone behind me. "Eva. Look."

I turned, following her line of sight. As soon as I noticed the woman clearing off another table behind us in this restaurant portion of the venue, I just barely refrained from gasping.

"Vanessa?" Nina said it as though she couldn't believe it. Stefan Giovanni's daughter wasn't someone we wanted to run into. She preyed on Dante, obsessive with trying to get him to marry her. Too late, we learned from my uncle that her father had set her up to it. Stefan pressured Vanessa to pursue Dante as another way of securing an alliance with the Constella name. My uncle was stubbornly lacking interest in her, even before he met Nina. Once he had, he was livid that Vanessa wouldn't give him up.

The tall woman lifted her face, frowning in fear at Nina's voice.

Oh, shit. A few yards separated us, but I saw the evidence of what she vainly tried to hide. Makeup could only go so far in covering bruises and cuts. Seeing this woman—once a peer of mine and a fellow "Mafia princess"—was sobering.

Someone had beaten her, and badly. She showed fear as she glanced around, as though she worried someone was watching her. Her gait suggested a limp as she approached our table.

"Eva?" she frowned at me, so skittish and nervous.

I wasn't shocked that she referenced me. She'd known me—or of me—the longest.

"What happened?" I asked. It wasn't a great greeting, but it made the most sense. I didn't want to chat with her. She would never be an acquaintance of mine again, not after the way she chased after my uncle.

"I... I..." She looked around again, so scared of the guests and diners in here. Maybe she was looking for the Constella guards who stayed near the back of the room. I couldn't tell, but she was terrified. She barely spared Nina and Tessa a glance. Instead, she singled me out.

"What happened?"

Her beaten appearance was startling enough. But the fact that she was working *here* as a common low-income employee didn't add up.

"I ran. I had to." She licked her lips, so nervous. "I... ran from home."

"Why?" Nina asked. Even though she had every right to loathe this woman who tried to steal her man, she wasn't cold.

"I had to. I had to run from my father." She looked back at me, singling me out again. "He's hellbent on ruining the Constella organization." Now, she glanced at Nina, furrowing her brow. "He's furious that Dante wouldn't help them."

I huffed. "Tough shit."

Vanessa nodded, a nervous motion. "After the alliance with the Domino Family was broken up, Stefan's been so desperate to secure backing. To recoup his losses."

I shook my head. "He's never touching a cent of the Constella wealth. Or any bit of power."

"But he's still so desperate." Vanessa glanced around again. "And you shouldn't be out here, dining out and having fun. Your guards need to be closer." She licked her lips, cringing as she touched the split in the lower one. "You need to watch your backs."

"No, we don't. Our men will always do that for us." Tessa tipped her chin up, defiant.

Vanessa sighed. "You'd better hope they can. Stefan's been siding with those MC assholes, and they're hard men. Brutal men."

I assumed she meant that literally, given her broken appearance. Before I could feel sorry for her, I honed in on getting intel.

"Are you saying that with firsthand experience?"

Vanessa sniffed. "I am. Stefan offered to give me to them in lieu of a payment overdue for guns. And they…"

Nina shook her head. "What a sick motherfucker." She reached into her purse and pulled out cash.

"Nina. No."

She sneered at my warning. Then she shoved some money to Vanessa.

"This isn't Constella money going to a Giovanni," she sassed. "She's not with them."

Vanessa blinked back tears. "I'm not with anyone. And if I can run far and fast enough, I'll never go near my father or his new friends ever again." She folded the cash and quickly shoved it into her pocket. "I'd rather die than see any of them. They're not like the Mafia soldiers." Again, she faced me, almost as though she respected that I wanted details. "They're ruthless. Selling women. Violating them. I lasted two nights in their clubhouse before I could escape."

I firmed my lips and shook my head, furious that men like those bikers could get away with operating where we always had. Dante didn't traffic humans, and I suspected that was why he steered clear of the Devil's Brothers and Stefan when he started to favor them.

"Then go. Get the fuck out of here," I said as I gave her cash from my purse.

"Thank you. Thank you so much." She pocketed it too, crying outright now. "And you need to tell him. Tell your uncle. Tell your soldiers. Stefan is teaming up with those bikers, and I'm not sure who will be able to take them both on."

I nodded. "Go."

She lingered, glancing at us all. "They have a second compound, too."

I perked up, listening for something useful. "Where?"

She described the location, apologizing that she couldn't be more accurate. "I was so scared when I escaped. I... I was worried they'd broken my leg. But it's in that area."

"Thank you." I stood, urging Nina and Tessa to get up. I had to take this information straight to my uncle.

As our guards approached, I held my hand up to stop them from getting too close. "Go," I ordered Vanessa. "Go now."

She didn't need to be told twice. Turning hastily, she limped away.

"Eva." Tony, one of the guards, started after her. "Is that Miss—"

"No." I shook my head. "She's no threat to us." While she was manipulative before, I knew this wasn't a trap. I saw the wounds and knew she couldn't be faking it. The Vanessa I knew before never would've stooped to accept cash as charity. "Let her go."

Tony narrowed his eyes at me, but I stood firm. Bringing Vanessa to us would cause more problems. Dante would want to kill her. Stefan could use her being captured by us as a reason to attack. Any number of undesirable consequences could follow.

"Get us home. Now." I strode for the door, eager to share this news with my uncle. If this detail could put us in a better position against our enemies, then I would hurry it along.

Because the fewer enemies we had building up against us like this, the more likely I could achieve a future with Liam and Olivia.

19

LIAM

Yesterday, I spent hours with Franco and another new recruit getting fitted for suits. It was a far cry from the uniform I was used to in the military, but I wasn't going to protest the Constella dress code.

Eva enjoyed checking me out in my tailored garments last night, too.

However, tonight, on my first official assignment, I was dressed down in the shittiest jeans I owned and a plain black T-shirt.

Just like I wouldn't complain or criticize how they wanted me to dress in an expensive suit, I wouldn't say no to anything they asked me to do. Including going undercover to this second, secret MC compound where they wanted me to place a listening device. Recording the conversations that the bikers held in privacy would give Dante and the Constella forced much-needed intel to remain ahead of the game. I understood that Dante, Romeo, and Franco all kept themselves in a position to stay one step ahead of the Giovannis and the Devil's Brothers, and I respected that they weren't rash gangster idiots.

They strategized just like my superiors had in the army, and it was no different. Not the same battlefield, but the same concepts were at the base of it all.

Dante approached me near the garage, where I was getting fitted with different guns. He nodded, approving of how I looked. "I agree," he told Franco. "Looking like this, he's the most likely to get close enough undetected."

That was all I had to do. Sneak in, plant the bug, and get out. Easy, peasy.

"Well, they would be able to identify most of our men," Romeo said, also looking me over. He was always so serious, but I wanted to tell him that I had this. This was far from the first undercover task I'd completed.

"And he hasn't been around for long."

I grunted a laugh as they checked my holsters. "I can't believe it's only been a month." It felt like so long ago since Eva and I met at that engagement party. Now, after all these weeks when we'd tried to keep our distance, we were together.

"Are you ready?" Franco asked. He was the supervisor I reported to, the highest-ranking capo in the organization. Although he was the man I had to directly answer to, he seemed more like a friend than a manager. Every night this past week, after dinner and before I'd wait for Eva to come to my room, we hung out over a drink and just talked.

"It *is* kind of quick," he said of my first assignment arriving.

"Nah. I'm good. Just need to check on my girls." I stopped midstep. "Girl," I corrected. It was too damn easy to see Eva and Olivia as my *girls*, plural. But I had yet to tell any of these men that I was sleeping with her. I got the impression she wanted to keep it on the down low too, and until we agreed that we'd make it known, I'd follow her lead.

Lots of things were happening right now, and I didn't want to complicate anything by telling Dante that I was with his precious niece. I was no one, an outsider fitting in. If anyone claimed I wasn't worthy or good enough for the Mafia princess, I had no grounds to argue it. I would, but I understood my position here, and technically, I was nothing more than a guest who overstayed my stay until I became a new hire.

I didn't look back to see if the men heard my slip. Or if they noticed. No one called me out for the way I implied that Eva was my girl. Instead, staying punctual to the assignment, I headed to my room where Olivia was still napping. Eva had fallen asleep in my bed, but I didn't want to presume anything.

"Hey," I said after I entered, finding her walking out of the shower.

"Hey." She smiled. "Getting ready to leave?" She looked over my grungy outfit.

"Yeah. But I wanted to stop in and say bye."

"Oh." She ran her hand through her hair. "Is Danicia coming to babysit, then? I'll get out of the way."

I grabbed her at her side, giving in to the temptation to slide my hand under the towel and caress her smooth skin. I couldn't get enough of her, and I was weak to want to touch her every chance I could.

"You are."

She frowned. "I'm in the way?"

"No." I kissed her. "You're babysitting. Or I'm hoping you will."

Her smile lifted my heart. She was goddamn gorgeous when she grinned like this, that private, soft smile just for me. "You want me to watch Olivia?"

I nodded. "Yeah. You're spending so much time with me—and her—it makes sense, right?"

She was still surprised, pleasantly, but she agreed with a nod. "Well, yeah. I wouldn't mind at all."

"Good." I kissed her again, then looked her over with a long sigh. "But don't wait up for me."

She rolled her eyes. "As if." She dropped the towel and turned to get her clothes.

"You tease."

She rubbed her hands over her bare ass, taunting me more as she bent over. "Go on. Be careful and come back to me." She glanced toward the crib. "To us."

Damn, I liked the sound of that. Not just me and her, but all three of us. I'd never considered being a father, but now that I was, I was a package deal. And she'd accepted both me and my daughter.

I left before I'd been tempted to go after her, and as I rode out on a bike Dante secured for me—not mine, since the MC might recognize it after some of the men picked a fight with me at that gas station—I savored the allure of coming back to Eva. And Olivia.

I had something to fight for, more than ever, and with that reminder, I was motivated to be alert and focus on this first assignment.

The ride to the area where this second compound was didn't appeal. It was a rundown part of the city, neglected and beaten down with the pressure from weather, lack of maintenance, and gangs. Squatters no doubt stayed in many of the structures barely standing upright, and I knew I had to be in the right place when more motorcycle engines roared in the distance. I stopped my bike near a bar, but I didn't go inside. Now that I knew what the Devil's Brothers' cuts looked like, their patches and emblem, I could spot them and avoid their noticing me.

The compound wasn't too hidden, not with the music blaring from inside. A party—or three—raged on in there, and with the cover of blending in with other bikers, I slipped into the rundown building.

At one time, it was likely a warehouse. Tonight, it was a shot-up dump. The grimy interior didn't stop the bikers and whores from drinking, taking drugs, and dancing. Weaving through the crowd wasn't as easy as I'd hoped.

Too many glances at me made me nervous, even with the sham replica of the Devil's Brothers' cut on my back. The leather of the sleeveless vest was still stiff, unused and not broken into since Franco had someone stitch it together this afternoon.

But it worked. My disguise covered me all the way toward the back of the building. Franco, Romeo, and a spy named Andy all strategized with me earlier. Placing the spyware in the main clubhouse wouldn't be effective with the risk of multiple conversations overlapping or music droning voices out.

Back here, near smaller rooms where people could speak without distractions, were more optimal places to stick the small recording devices.

As long as they don't sweep this place for bugs, I mused after I put three in smaller rooms. They were all empty, but I bet they held meetings and "church" in here. Each room had a main table and chairs set out for an audience. One looked like an office, maybe where Reaper held phone calls.

"Hey!"

I stopped short at the sound of a man noticing me in the hallway.

"Yeah, man?" I talked casually, turning and using the beer bottle I'd grabbed as a prop. I lifted it for a drink in case he'd recognize my face.

"Where you going? You ain't supposed to be by the Prez's office."

I shrugged. "Just took a piss and walking the long way back to the whores."

He grinned, showing me his gnarly, stained teeth. "You want a piece of the new one we got tonight?" He tipped his head toward another door that I hadn't tried yet. "Get in there before she passes out, man. They're so fucking hot when they cry."

I gritted my teeth, resisting the urge to attack this asshole. In the main clubhouse, the whores seemed into it. They were likely the usual ones they kept here. But in the back?

Maybe that's where those screams are coming from.

"Yeah, man. Take a look." The biker held open the door, giving me a preview of the three young women being gang-raped. All holes were filled. Blood and cum dripped over their flesh. With their sounds of protest at being restrained and raped, my soul hardened and darkened.

They were teens, not even women yet, and the urge to kill all of these sick fucks nearly overwhelmed me.

I wouldn't survive it. One man against dozens was suicide, and I had Eva and Olivia to live for. I had to get back to them, but I swore on my soul that these motherfuckers would die slow, painful deaths.

I slipped away, claiming the need for more booze first. As soon as that biker left me and I wove through the crowds again, I let my fury bottle inside me.

You sick assholes. Raping young girls. It was a crime, an atrocity, and it killed me to have to walk away.

I'd placed all the recording devices that I had, and with confidence that I'd successfully pulled off my mission, I left the compound.

Bothered, no, enraged, by what I saw, I walked back to where I'd left my bike. *At least the girls at home are safe.* Nina, Tessa, and Eva were all accounted for and thoroughly protected. While the men in the Constella family were killers, they weren't rapists like these nasty bikers.

Comparing the two evils, I felt better about my choice to work for Dante. My views on the Mafia had changed since I told Dante that I'd be his soldier, but seeing the gang rapes in that compound served as further evidence that I'd sided with the lesser of two evils.

As I approached the bike, I slowed in my steps.

"What the *fuck* do you think you're doing?" a Devil's Brothers biker asked as he stalked toward me.

He stood between me and the borrowed motorcycle, blocking me from escaping.

"With that motherfucking fake cut you got on," another biker added, flicking his fingers at his own leather vest.

Both toted knives, eyeing me like I'd be carved up in seconds.

Goddammit. Just when I'd been thinking I had gone undetected.

"You a spy? Huh? What the fuck are you doing on our property?"

I pulled in a deep breath, bracing myself to fight my way out of here.

Because I was leaving. They wouldn't keep me here. I had Eva and Liv to come home to, and no one was stopping me.

I grabbed my gun and fired at them.

20

EVA

"Look at you go," I exclaimed on my hands and knees in the great room. I sat back, grinning at the adorable toddler coming toward me.

Olivia giggled and walked faster, her chest up, arms out, and her smile huge. "Go. Go. Go."

"Yeah, you're on the go," Nina said as Liv crashed into me, cuddling instantly. "She was cruising yesterday, and now she's everywhere!"

"You figured out it's faster than crawling, huh?" I asked the little girl who yawned on my lap.

"And more tiring." I scooped her up in my arms, confident I'd never tire of her sweet, clean baby smell. And these little, itty-bitty hands squeezing my fingers. They were just so small, and soon, she'd grow up so fast.

I wonder if Liam is sad about all the time he's already missed with her. Not even knowing she existed. "You know," I told Nina, who came to hang out with me and Olivia, "it's pretty lousy of Pamela to never have told Liam that he was a father."

She smirked, nodding. "I know. He had a right to be informed, even if it wasn't in line with what she thought he'd want."

I shook my head, hating that she'd hidden her from her father. He might not have planned to be a father yet—or at all—but he'd adapted to being Liv's daddy so quickly that it was hard to imagine his ever not being a father. He was clueless in the stores when we shopped that one day, but hell, the baby industry *was* overwhelming. I said that with my limited expertise in helping Nina arrange her baby registry.

Every day, he doted on her, and every night, he probably could sit back and realize he'd learned so much more about her, himself, and what parenthood entailed.

And he'd never complain. He'd never take any moment back and regret that he had Liv in his life.

Which makes me love you all the more. I sighed, knowing I was falling for him so quickly.

Nina misinterpreted my sigh. "You're worried about him, aren't you?"

I smiled at Olivia as she batted at my hair. "Yes and no. It's nothing different from worrying about Uncle Dante. Romeo. Franco. All the men who serve to protect us. Yet…" I grimaced. "I am."

"You two have really hit it off. Quickly."

But profoundly too. "I'm not worried because I know he—like all the others I just mentioned—is trained and qualified for the work they do. Liam was a soldier. He's received specialized practice with dangerous situations."

She nodded. "But…"

I sighed again, hugging Olivia close. "But I am nervous. I've only just found him. And we've only just gotten together and figured out that we can try to make this work between us."

"It's new. And scary." She stood, patting my shoulder. "You're allowed to feel both ends of the spectrum about it."

"Yeah." I smiled at her as she yawned. "If I didn't have this one to preoccupy me all night, I'm sure I would be more stressed."

Nina grinned as I picked up an also yawning Olivia. "I bet. She's sure keeping you on your toes tonight."

We parted ways, for the tired mama-to-be to rest and wait up for Dante and for me to take an even sleepier Olivia to Liam's room. She was already bathed, so it was just a matter of reading her a story. The little toddler was already so close to sleeping that she couldn't last until the end of the book, but I stayed in the chair for a longer while, taking the comfort her small, warm body offered me.

Okay. If I don't put her in the crib now, she'll be more likely to wake when I move her later.

Gingerly, holding my breathing and getting out of the chair as slowly as I could, I transferred her to the crib.

She didn't stir, and I smiled down at her. It seemed that I sure tired her out with all that playing around. I only hoped she'd stay asleep when Liam came home and he—or we—wouldn't need to coax her to fall back asleep. She could be a light sleeper or a deep one, and I wasn't sure if there was a method to figure out which mode came when.

I tried to relax in Liam's bed for the rest of the night, keeping watch over Olivia. Scrolling on my phone didn't entertain me for long, but playing mindless games on it almost distracted me from the worry that escalated and intensified with each passing moment.

Liam was qualified. He wasn't reckless. I *knew* he was capable of anything Franco assigned him to do, but the longer I waited and fretted that it was getting so late—

The door opened. I burst up from the bed and let my phone fall on the mattress. "Liam," I whispered as I hurried to him.

He exhaled in relief at the sight of me, but he held up his hand to stop me from hugging him. "Let me... Let me clean up first."

Covered in blood and grime, he looked a mess. But I knew better than to fuss. I nodded. "Did you report to Dante or Franco?"

He nodded, then tilted his head toward the bathroom. A glance at Olivia showed him that she was fast asleep. He took my hand and led me to follow him into the other room.

I didn't close the door all the way in case Liv cried out, but I pushed it almost shut so she wouldn't be bothered by the noise or light.

"I put the devices in the compound," he said as he lifted his shirt. A deep wince marred his face, though, and I reached closer to help him.

Together, we peeled off his clothes and I did my best not to grimace at the signs of injuries on him.

"But on my way out, they realized I was a spy."

"Fuck," I mumbled.

I lowered to help get his jeans off, his boxers too. Even though this man would always turn me on, it wasn't the time for anything sensual or sexy. He leaned on me, setting his hands on my shoulders to balance himself as he stepped out of his boots. Once he was upright, inspecting the gash on his bicep, I started the shower for him.

"They ambushed me at the bike," he said as he stepped into the shower. "I killed the one who shot at me. But it wasn't good odds."

I frowned as I gathered his clothes into a bundle to dispose of later. "How many?"

"Four in the end." He groaned slightly under the water, and I shushed him, hearing Olivia in the other room.

After I checked on her and helped her keep her pacifier in her mouth, I returned to him just as he stepped out of the shower. "Let me help you with that," I said.

He sighed, too tired to put up a fight, and wrapped the towel around his waist. I guided him to sit on the vanity, and once he was in place, I compressed the graze on his arm and bandaged it. All the while, he was quiet and still. I felt the heat of his stare on me, but it wasn't a smoldering expression of desire. Just one of appreciation. Gratitude. Maybe something a lot like love.

"Stay with me." He took my free hand and held it. "Stay with me tonight."

I smiled slyly, hoping I could lighten the moment a bit. "I know you said that you wanted me to wait up for you, but I think you need sleep more than sex."

He winced as he stood. "I think you're right." He tugged off my shirt and kissed me softly. "But I mean you to stay. To sleep with me."

His sincere tone wasn't a ploy. He wasn't trying to get in my pants. All he wanted was for me to sleep over instead of sneaking back to my wing in the house like I typically did.

I shivered with the lack of warmth from the long-sleeved shirt he removed. As he tugged at my shorts, I followed suit and lowered them. In a cami and panties, I walked with him to the bed and watched him climb in.

Before I joined him, I checked once more on Olivia. She was sound asleep, content, but I was glad to stay the night. If she woke and needed help, it'd be my honor to let Liam rest and not have to tend to her for once.

"Come here." He held his arm up, welcoming me in to be spooned by his hard, hot body.

Nestled together, we sighed in unison. I smiled in the darkness, closing my eyes to savor his body flush to mine. After a gentle kiss on the top of my head, he yawned. "Thank you for watching her tonight."

"Thank you for letting me." I turned slightly to kiss his cheek. "Rest, Liam. I'll be right here for whatever you need."

I turned back to my side as he hugged me close, and I loved how I could tell him that and know he'd understand that I meant it in every way. Not just as a girlfriend or lover to satisfy him sexually, but as a partner in all life had to offer.

21

LIAM

The minute I came to my room and saw Eva, I relaxed. After a glance at the crib to show me that Olivia was safe and sound, sleeping away, I could finally exhale the breath I'd been holding all night.

They were protected here. Unlike those girls at the Devil's Brothers' compound.

All the aches and pains faded. The agony spreading over my skin from where the bullet grazed me no longer stung as badly.

One glimpse of my future—Eva and Olivia—and I was grounded again.

I fought for them. I was determined to succeed because of them. When those bikers ganged up on me, when I realized things were getting dicey, they were my motivation to punch, kick, and deflect faster and better. And I had.

Thank fuck. I'd never been happier to be back from a mission, and it was a pivotal moment of knowing that I had my reason. Enlisting in and staying in the army was a generalized act of servitude. Here, as a Constella spy and soldier, I had my reason right here in front of me.

Eva didn't get emotional about my wounds and injuries. With a calm manner, she tended to me exactly how I needed. Words weren't necessary. She got it. She saw what I'd endured and no questions would be asked. It was easy to accept her help, and as I fell asleep, I drifted with the fact that I could trust her. That she would always listen to my report and sympathize. That she would always know that shit could turn south and that she'd step up to the challenge and nurture me until I was back in charge like I preferred to be.

In the morning, I woke up late. Franco scheduled me around other expectations—like the need to rest and recover after the risky assignment last night. He also knew that I'd be at Nina's baby shower later today, like many other soldiers.

But sleeping in was still a rarity. Olivia usually woke me up.

Not today.

Eva sat next to me on the bed, playing a form of silent peek-a-boo with Liv, who smiled back at her instead of playing with the stuffed animal between them.

Instead of sneaking back to her room last night, Eva stayed with me. She slept over, and I wasn't going to ignore how big of a step that was for us. This wasn't the first time she'd stayed in my bed, but it was usually for a nap, not to wake up with me in the morning.

Now that she had, now that I had the supreme pleasure of opening my eyes and seeing her as the person to greet me first thing, I wasn't sure I could ever go back to not having her in my bed.

"Morning." I cleared my throat and watched as they both looked over at me. It was a cozy, gentle moment for the three of us, and I wanted to be lazy and savor every second of it.

"Can you tell Daddy *good morning*?" Eva repeated it slowly a couple more times.

"Hi!" Olivia pushed her hand to her mouth and released it, blowing a kiss. "Hi!"

Eva and I laughed lightly at her enthusiasm.

"Hi!" Eva replied in kind, tickling her as Liv smiled.

Seeing them together was a treat, and if I hadn't already reached the point of being utterly besotted with this generous woman, I definitely was now.

It was a huge change from what I knew before. When I met Eva, she was so aloof and stiff, icy and quick to cast judgment. Looking at her now, I respected that she'd shifted with my arrival in her life.

"Eva?"

She didn't look at me. She only had eyes for Olivia as my daughter lunged at her and kissed her face. On both cheeks, her nose, her brow, her chin, then everywhere again. Over and over, like a bird pecking, and it elicited giggles from both of them. "Yeah?" she asked when she could manage a moment to speak.

I wasn't immune to the laughter. I chuckled along as I shifted on the pillows to accommodate the ache in my upper back.

"How come you were so icy when we met?"

She sighed. "*That's* the burning question you want an answer to right now?"

"You're just so…" I brushed her hair back to see her face clearer. Olivia slumped to her chest, hugging her, but she grabbed hold of my hand before I could lower it. She traced the calloused areas and lines of scars on my hand.

"It's not you. I'm looking at you now, happy and open and so good with her." I shook my head. "This is the real you. Why did you need to hide behind a front and act so cold when we met?"

She shrugged, not denying it or protesting. "It's a defense mechanism."

"Be hard and tough at the first interaction, then maintain it until you can lower your guard?" I guessed.

"That sounds about right." She sighed deeply, gazing at me.

I loved that she wasn't offended or irritated that I was asking about this.

"Last night, you were on the frontlines of danger. You saw how much the family relies on physical defense against our enemies. I've always been prepared for managing and staying strong against other levels of enemies. We don't only get attacked. Someone is always out there waiting to lie to us, to manipulate us, and to con us. I was raised to always expect the worst and prepare for it." She smiled at Olivia, then leaned in to kiss me. "But I don't count on the worst from you two. Only good times. A bright future."

I rose up on my elbow and kissed her for longer. "Then maybe we shouldn't waste so much time trying to hide it anymore."

Her answering grin blinded me. "Yeah?"

I nodded. "We can go to this baby party—"

"Baby shower," she corrected with a lopsided smile.

"Together. No more trying to pretend we're not sleeping together."

"I don't want to burst your bubble, but Tessa and Nina caught on quick."

I rolled my eyes. That didn't surprise me, especially not after the night Tessa let herself into my room to tell me about the security concerns. "And it's probably safe to assume that what Tessa and Nina know, so do Dante and Romeo."

"Yep. Pretty much. They don't keep secrets."

I lifted her hand and kissed her knuckles. "And neither will we. From each other or the rest of them."

Later, at the frou-frou tea time place, we did exactly that. I carried Olivia in, crushing her fluffy tea party dress as I held her at my left side. At my right, Eva held my hand and walked with us. We showed up as a couple, as a little unit of three, and there was no way anyone wouldn't understand I was with her, that she was with me, and both of us would support Olivia.

I wasn't expected to stand by here as a soldier on guard, but it was impossible not to. While Eva and Olivia sat around with the other women, I stayed back along the wall with several of the men. It was a couples thing, not just the women invited. When I asked Eva why this baby shower included men on the guest list, she said that it made the most sense. All the women here would have equally overprotective guards and significant others nearby, so why not simplify it?

It sounded controlling, that these Mafia women could never go anywhere alone or have independence, but it was simply a fact of life for them. They were the daughters, sisters, girlfriends, and wives of powerful men, and like Eva explained, everyone would fight or sneak their way into taking that power and money for themselves.

Multiple other soldiers were positioned around the room, in and out of it, so I wasn't nervous about anyone breaking in and causing issues.

After the stressful night I had at the Devil's Brothers' compound, I was glad for a chance to just be, to relax and smile at Eva and Olivia partying. They played games. We all had food. Olivia walked everywhere, stunning me with how quickly she was mastering the fine art of seeming to be all over the place at once.

Still, as I stood back with the other men, we shifted to talking about business, about work.

"It's not in vain," Franco argued with me when I complained about the recording devices being found and destroyed at the compound.

"How is it not? I snuck in there to place the bugs, and they found them immediately."

Andy, the soldier Romeo often relied on to spy on the bikers, shrugged. "It's just the way it is. They sweep for bugs constantly. They're paranoid motherfuckers."

"So if I went back another time, they'd find them again?" I asked. I wasn't volunteering, but curious.

"Yeah." Andy smirked. "Just like the first two times I tried to record anything at their main clubhouse."

I sighed, shaking my head at the slight failure. They weren't blaming me, but I held myself accountable, anyway.

"And it might not be necessary," Romeo chimed in. "My father and I are hoping that things will come to a head sooner than later with both of them. Stefan and Reaper won't last as partners for long. They're both too greedy and volatile." He glanced at me. "If we play this right, they'll cancel each other out and spare us having to lose any men in this war."

That would be an ideal outcome. Fewer casualties. Less destruction of property. I was all in favor of that.

"Hey," Eva said as she approached with Olivia in her arms. She was fussing, but that could easily be fixed. "Do you know where—"

I pointed at where I'd set Olivia's bottle on a nearby table. She was doing her hungry fuss, and any minute now, she'd be cranky because she was tired. I was damned proud of myself for knowing how to read her so well.

"Perfect. Thanks." She hoisted her higher on her hip.

"She'll get sleepy," I reminded her.

She nodded. "Yeah. And I'll bring her to you to hold. My arm's about to fall off." It might have sounded like a complaint, but with her smile, it was more like a joke. When the mood struck, Olivia could cling.

"I'll be waiting." Before she walked off, I snagged her close and kissed her.

"You didn't wait long," Franco teased.

"Long for what?" I asked.

"To sleep with the boss's niece." Franco chuckled at Romeo, rolling his eyes.

"And you call yourself head of security?" Romeo joked. "They were fucking before we hired him."

Franco raised his brows, still amused, and I merely shrugged. They could have their entertainment.

We all laughed it off, and I was damned glad that Eva and I had come out as a couple here. Like I suspected, everyone already knew that we had something going on. All those weeks of sexual tension had to have given us away.

Now that we'd taken another step forward to a real relationship, I appreciated their support.

Even if we didn't have it, if anyone protested in the family, I would've fought for her.

I always would.

22

EVA

For the first time in my life, I had a routine. Liam and I developed one with Olivia, and I wasn't sure how I could claim that I was living before they came here.

Two months ago, I felt like I needed a job. I told Franco that I wanted a purpose.

Never in a million years could I have anticipated finding my purpose in the little toddler who seemed to grow quicker than I could blink.

And I wouldn't change it for the world. Olivia tapped something in me. Something maternal and deep, like I didn't *have* to hide as much as I had been. That it was okay not to be so defensive all the time. It didn't need to be my default. Because getting to know Olivia and watching after her when Liam was working, it felt wrong to help raise her and teach her to always be on guard.

I understood why Uncle Dante raised me the way he did. He didn't know better. He was a struggling single parent, doing the best he could with Romeo since my aunt passed away when he was a baby.

Uncle Dante had done his best with what he knew at the time. Raising a strong generation was a must, but by the time he softened his parenting methods when Romeo and I were teens, it was too late to change the course for me. Romeo grew up to be too serious. And I grew up to be icy and defensive, closing my heart to anyone.

So it wasn't a shocker that Oliva and Liam could thaw me out. They had my heart, and I wondered if I was being too giddy and ignorant to trust that it could last. It seemed too peaceful, too easy, to become something like a second mom to Olivia. And that niggling worry of something bound to fall apart kept me slightly less engaged at lunch one afternoon.

"Your house was finished two weeks ago," Uncle Dante reminded me.

I nodded and glanced at Liam. "It was. But it might not be the best place for Olivia." Too many stairs. Too many floors. As a single woman, it suited me fine. But it wasn't the homiest place for a family.

Liam's slow and sexy smile melted my heart. He had to be thinking the same thing, that we *were* a little family unit.

I wasn't sure how anyone could assume otherwise. I stayed in his guest suite. We slept together every night, woke up together in the morning except if he had to handle something for Franco. I liked watching Olivia, and no one questioned that I would. We were already acting like a family within a bigger one.

"Are you trying to kick me out or something?" I teased my uncle.

Romeo and Tessa had finally moved back to the house they were slowly renovating, but when we had late nights, they still stayed in their wing here.

"Never," Uncle Dante promised. "But I understand the need for space."

Liam chuckled. "Like there's not enough of that here."

"With the baby stuff. Livy's older," Uncle Dante said with a smile for her as she batted her spoon on her plate and fisted the food she was eating, "but it all adds up."

Nina nodded. "It already seems like so much more space is lost with the bassinet and changing table and crib and…" She blew out a breath, exaggerating her run-on. "Letting Olivia have her own room would be smart. And while she can have a room here, wouldn't it be helpful to let her acclimate to *her* room, permanently?"

I sighed, both hating this topic and appreciating her insight. I knew what she meant. Olivia slept on her own in her crib, but it was still so close to where Liam and I slept. Moving Olivia into her *own* room was a big step, and it would be wise to do so where she'd call home—if this mansion wouldn't stay her place.

"Having privacy would be nice," Liam quipped dryly.

Tessa groaned from across the table. "I walked in *one* time…"

Romeo shook his head. "No. I did too. I thought you took Eva and Nina with you to the yoga studio and went to talk with him." He cleared his throat and looked anywhere but at me and Liam. "Again. I suggest you *lock* the door next time…"

Liam rolled his eyes. "Next time? You presume to enter without waiting for a reply again?"

Franco held his hands up. "Okay, okay. I think we've all made our points here. Some spacing out wouldn't be bad with you all shacking up and getting busy. All I suggest is that we plan security in line with who's living where."

"What about you?" Liam asked. He wasn't teasing or mean, but intrigued as he looked at Franco. "How come the family's highest-ranking capo is still a bachelor?"

I kicked his leg under the table, hoping to warn him to shut up.

Franco smirked and looked off to the side. Romeo hissed, leaning forward to rub his shin.

Whoops. I kicked the wrong leg. "What the hell, Eva?"

"What the *heck*," Nina corrected.

Dante chuckled. "Nina, every baby in this house is going to hear things they shouldn't."

She pursed her lips. "That doesn't mean we can't try to tone it down."

"What the heck!" Olivia exclaimed with a huge smile.

Nina gestured at her, triumphant. "See!"

"Heck hell," Olivia added, thinking she was on a roll.

Nina deadpanned.

I leaned toward her. "Now say *dang it*, not *damn—*"

She laughed and elbowed my side. "Oh, stop."

After lunch, without Liam or me making concrete plans to move anywhere, I walked Olivia back to his room to get her dressed for swimming. Uncle Dante found a swim instructor for her, and I only had ten minutes before the lesson would start. Liam was due to leave with Franco, but he caught up to me despite already having kissed us both good bye.

"Hey, wait up," he said in the hallway. "Why was that such a bad question? When I asked Franco why he was single."

I glanced at him, worried about being late. These swim lessons were Olivia's favorite.

"It wasn't a bad question, per se. He prefers not to talk about it," I replied.

"Talk about *what*, though?" He frowned, helping me with Olivia as I reached for her bathing suit and swim diaper. "I'd like to think that Franco and I are becoming good friends. We talk quite a bit. He's more than a supervisor."

I nodded, agreeing, because I noticed that too. "I can tell. He is opening up to you, but he doesn't talk about Chloe with very many people." I huffed. "I bet Romeo forgot her name."

"Chloe? Who is she? Or was she?" He cringed. "Was she killed?"

"No." I shrugged. "I'm guessing she's still alive. Franco was really serious about her back when he was young, but she didn't want to stay with him, and that heartbreak never healed."

"Damn." He shook his head. "So it's a bitter topic I should avoid then, huh?"

I nodded. "Maybe. Or let him bring it up to you." It'd been years since Franco and Chloe were a thing, but it seemed that he really struggled to let her go. "When and if he wants to talk about it."

"Thanks for the heads up." He kissed the top of Olivia's head, then gave me a longer lip lock. "As much as I enjoy the job security and I like this new gig, I value his friendship too. Tell me if I ever put my foot in my mouth again." He grinned, mischievous. "Or aim for *my* leg when you're kicking it under the table next time."

I laughed, watching him leave.

The swim lesson was another success, and throughout it, I was so busy watching and helping Olivia that the conversations from lunchtime fell to the back burner. Once we left, headed back up to Liam's room so I could change Olivia, I realized that having a pool—or pools, one indoor and outdoor—would be a plus. Uncle Dante would always welcome us here, and he enjoyed swimming with Olivia too, when he had the time, but Liam was right. Privacy would be nice. Real privacy to solidify ourselves as a growing family.

Because if he ever thought about putting a ring on my finger... I sighed, smiling at Olivia toddling faster and faster ahead of me.

I hurried to catch up to her, distracted when the front door opened. Roberto, one of the house guards, furrowed his brow as he entered. "Miss Constella."

I stopped, catching Olivia and holding her hand. "Yes?" I swung Olivia a little, the way she liked, just a back and forth swag of our joined hands. Then she leaped up to be held, and I carried her closer to the guard.

As he stepped inside, a woman appeared behind him. The tall redhead seemed so pale and thin that I wondered if she was ill, but she'd paid for some work to be done. Cosmetic beauty was nothing to shame, but my God, she could at least hire *quality* work.

"That's my niece," she accused, holding her head up high.

"Excuse me?"

I looked from this stranger to Roberto, trying to figure out why he'd let a stranger this far onto the property. He seemed confused but not intimidated. Diligent to his duties, he remained on alert and positioned himself between me and the woman.

"Who are you?" I demanded. Without an introduction coming from Roberto, I realized I'd need to demand answers myself.

Because there's no way in hell you are Olivia's aunt. She bore no resemblance to her. Liam said Pamela was an only child. And Liam didn't have siblings. Not even a cousin.

"She showed up at the gate, insisting that she's the legal guardian to Olivia." Roberto frowned at Olivia, as though he worried that she'd be taken away.

"That's bullshit." I hugged her closer.

"This isn't," the woman sneered, waving a document in the air. "That's my sister's baby, and I'll be damned if you try to kidnap her from me."

I tilted my head, instructing Roberto to get the paper from her. I wasn't inclined to hand over Olivia, not even if that birth certificate proved anything. Olivia was Liam's daughter, and he would be her guardian.

"I don't think so," the woman snapped, wrenching the paper out of Roberto's reach.

"Then fuck off," I said without any attempt to be polite or patient.

"You can't tell me to leave."

"I just did. If you have any legal claim to this girl, then you wouldn't be afraid to let us see your so-called proof on that document."

"It's legit."

I narrowed my eyes. "Then why wouldn't you let him see the paper?"

"How do I know if he'd rip it and destroy it?" she sassed back. "Regardless," she said as she shoved the paper into her purse, "that little girl isn't *yours*, is she?"

"Wouldn't you already know that? If you're claiming to be the sister of the mother?"

She opened and closed her mouth. "Hand her over. She's not yours."

By blood, no. Olivia wasn't mine. I didn't give birth to her. But we were strengthening our bond. I *felt* like a motherly figure to Olivia, and she came to me as though she trusted me as a parental person to rely on.

"Do you really think you are in any position to tell *me* what to do?"

Another guard arrived at the door, and I handed Olivia over to him as he strode into the house as backup.

Stalking closer to the woman, I let my defenses rise. The anger and protective energy that swarmed within me wouldn't peter out anytime soon.

"Do you think you have any fucking power to walk in here and act like you'll decide how things will be?"

She didn't cower. She stayed right where she was, not budging, but I didn't miss the nervousness she couldn't hide. Her gaze darted around, as though she needed to mark an exit from my getting in her face. Her lips lowered as her haughty smirk weakened.

"Get the fuck out of here," I warned.

"That child isn't yours, no matter how much you want to pretend she is."

"I'm not pretending anything." I gripped her neck, forcing her to squawk in surprise. Her hands batted at my grip, but I didn't care. Keeping my fingers on her neck, I pushed her to walk back out.

Even though *she* couldn't have any right to Olivia, she knew about her. And anyone knowing Olivia was here was dangerous. No one should be targeting her as someone to take. No one should be using her as a pawn in some kind of game.

At once, I worried that this redhead was working for the Devil's Brothers, but she was too polished. *Did Stefan send her here to take Olivia as yet another way to attack us and strike against us?*

It didn't matter who she was working for. She wouldn't get past me. Despite my protectiveness over Olivia, her words hit a mark. They sank in and irked me, but I refused to show it.

I wasn't pretending anything with Olivia. We'd forged a connection. She trusted me, and I cherished her as though I would my own flesh and blood. But hearing someone suggest that I didn't have a legitimate claim on her wounded me.

As though Olivia couldn't belong here, with me.

"You can't—"

I growled, unable to keep my anger pent up and bottled in. No one told me what I could and couldn't do. Especially not this stranger. And not over anything to do with Olivia.

"Get the fuck out of here," I repeated. It was the last time I'd tell her. As I caught sight of Liam striding inside, serious and grim-faced as he caught the end of this interaction, I knew my backup was here. He would set this woman right.

Because he could testify that Olivia would never be leaving us. Nothing would break us up or stop us from starting a family.

23

LIAM

"What's going on?"

I tore my gaze from Eva pushing a thin redhead out the door.

Goddamn, was she fierce. She glared at this stranger, seething and livid. Whatever this woman had said or done, it wasn't welcomed here. Eva was a tough woman. She had her guard up all the time, and seeing her in "action" here was a hell of a turn on.

I knew she was strong. She didn't take shit from anyone, but I'd never really witnessed her turning her bold attitude on someone else.

"This bitch thinks she's Olivia's aunt."

I narrowed my eyes, looking over this rail-then redhead. At first glance, she seemed like an unhealthy crackhead, too thin and malnourished, stuck in an addiction that was ruining her from the inside out.

She did not, in any way, resemble my daughter. "She's not." I was fuming, enraged that anyone would dare to make a claim on Olivia. The night the bikers chased after me showed me that I could be seen as a target because of my affiliation. But I'd calmed myself out of assuming that Olivia would ever be targeted because she would never be without someone to protect her. Even when she was older, a child, then a teen, growing into her own person, she would never be without security. It would simply be a fact of life, one I would be careful with. I didn't want to keep her too sheltered, but I'd never slack in protecting her while I helped to protect the Constella Family.

Pamela didn't have any siblings, so it was impossible for this woman to claim she was Olivia's aunt. Even if a sibling existed out there somewhere, it wouldn't matter. I was Olivia's father. She was in my custody and always would be.

I looked at Roberto, not wanting to step on his toes. He was the patrolling guard, and this liar would be his responsibility.

With a curt nod, he took hold of the woman and marched her out of the house. The older guard who held Olivia while she handled this woman gave her to me. As he headed out to help Roberto deal with this woman, no doubt to question her thoroughly and kick her off the property, I closed the door behind him.

"Damn."

She scowled, still so furious. When she turned to the side, I realized that she was doing her best to control her anger and not show it to the point that she'd scare Olivia. My daughter was oblivious, babbling about swimming and dolphins in her sweet voice as she tried out all the words she hadn't mastered. But I respected my woman that much more. She was livid, furious, and likely eager to kill that woman for daring to come here and make up that aunt bullshit. Yet, she was aware of not projecting her mood on Olivia.

"I know." When she faced me again, she seemed a tad calmer. Her mask was on. She wore it when she didn't want to reveal her sentiments.

"The audacity of just coming here and thinking she can tell us such a load of bullshit like that."

I smiled. "No. I mean, damn. Look at you."

She furrowed her brow. "What?"

"You're so..." I took her hand and led her to my room.

"So what?" she asked, twining her fingers with mine.

"So protective. Fierce." I looked her over, letting her see how much I wanted her. "It's sexy as hell, Eva."

She pursed her lips, still so angry that she couldn't consider anything else.

"You'd make a good mother," I said, pulling her closer to kiss her before we reached my door.

"Oh, yeah?" she asked, softening a bit.

I nodded. "Yeah. It doesn't matter if Olivia isn't your daughter by blood. You're a mama bear around her."

She smiled, sighing at Olivia yawning in my arms. Swimming always tired her out, and I was damned glad that Eva had already cleaned up and changed her out of her swimsuit.

Her too, because as soon as Olivia was napping, I intended to show Eva what I meant.

"She's too precious not to protect," Eva said softly, watching me lay her down in her crib.

"She is." I stepped back, amazed at how quickly Liv could close her eyes and be so content and comfortable to doze so easily.

"But you..." I turned and took her hands, leading her back to the bed. "You stun me, Eva."

I sat, urging her to straddle me on the edge of the bed. Her smile was playful and teasing, and I fell that much further under the spell of wanting her. Of loving her.

"Just because I stood up for your daughter?" She traced her finger along my jaw.

"Not just because of that." I pulled her close to kiss her hard.

"Then how else do I stun you?"

She wasn't fishing for compliments. She didn't need to. But I played along. I would never neglect to give her what she wanted. If she was in the mood to be called my naughty slut, I'd do that. If she wanted a list of how she blew my mind, I'd give her that as well.

Standing up, I forced her to get to her feet. I peeled off her shirt, kissing her as she relaxed against me. Her fingers weren't idle as I worshiped her body with my lips, brushing them over her soft skin. She tugged at my shirt, working it off me.

"Like this," I said, lowering her right hand to my erection trapped in my pants. "You're so goddamn gorgeous, Eva. Body, mind, and soul."

She smiled, catching on to how much I wanted to praise her. I gripped her pants to push them down, loving how she kissed me so hungrily at the same time she shimmied out of her clothes.

"You're the kind of woman I want in my life. As my lover." I kissed her and rubbed my finger along her wet folds. She was already so aroused, a common, happy occurrence whenever our clothes came off.

"As your slut?" she asked, breathless as I stepped out of my pants and boxers.

Unencumbered now, I was free to enjoy her grip on my dick, stroking it confidently. "That too." I lowered to the bed, clutching the backs of her thighs as she crawled onto my lap.

She didn't wait, grinding against me and rubbing my dick over her slick entrance.

"And as the mother of my children," I said, speaking words I never thought I'd utter in my life. Watching her with Olivia was a beautiful thing. Catching her defending her was another point of proof that I could trust her with my future.

"The mother of Olivia?" she asked, her voice soft yet hopeful. Cautious too.

"And..." I guided her down onto my erection, relishing the tight squeeze as she seated herself on me. "Any brothers or sisters we could arrange for her."

"Mmm." She kept her moan low and quiet, but it didn't diminish the sexy sound at all. "Is this practice, then?" she asked as she lifted and sank back on me again.

"Yeah," I growled, cupping her breasts as she arched her back. "We should practice. All the time."

She smiled, a smug grin that taunted me. "We do practice all the time."

"Then we'll practice more."

We were playful and teasing, but the crux of this conversation was a big topic. A big deal. I meant every word, though. Starting a family with this woman was something I considered halfway done. She was the mother I wanted for Olivia. She was my partner. Sooner than later, we'd need to figure out where to live. I had ideas for a proposal, but I wanted to wait on it and ponder how to best ask her to marry me.

We hadn't known each other for long, but it was long enough. I knew. I wanted *her*, and no one else.

She came quickly, maybe too quickly as she rode me, but I wasn't upset. Slow or fast, we always got off with each other. As she tightened her pussy walls around me, I watched her breasts and admired the redness of my fingers tugging on those tasty nipples.

Next time. Next time, we'll play longer. Next time, I'll get my mouth on her. Next time...

I came, digging my fingers into her ass and slamming her down tight on me as I thrust up into her. My dick jerked, and as I unloaded my hot cum into her, I knew it wasn't a matter of *next time* with her.

I wanted her forever, for every day and night for the rest of our lives.

I need to make it happen. Regardless of how recently I'd come into her life and into this family's organization, I had to ensure that I stayed with her.

No interloper would dare to take *our* daughter. No enemy would threaten this new beginning I'd found here.

I'd swear on it, and I'd fight until my last breath to ensure it.

24

EVA

"She is just adorable," Jenny, the swim instructor, said after another fun lesson with Olivia. Liam's little girl had a knack for winning anyone and everyone over. Even during her tantrum-like moments. "You're doing good, Mama."

The older woman grinned at me and gave me a thumbs-up.

"Oh, but I'm not—"

"Nah, Eva. Don't sell yourself short. You've got a good balance between being a disciplinarian and giving encouragement. Not many first-time mothers can achieve that."

I was about to correct her that I wasn't Olivia's mother, but she'd misinterpreted my rejection of praise as though I thought I wasn't worthy of it. Every day, I struggled with the concept of not being the one to watch over Olivia. I was "only" Liam's girlfriend, a quasi-live-in one at that. I was also a relative of his employer. It was complicated, yet not. We were making it work.

Over the last few weeks, though, as the holidays came and went, I had a hunch that Liam was eager to really settle down with me. We shelved talking about moving for a while. It just made sense at the big mansion with Dante and Nina, and sometimes with Romeo and Tessa. We relocated Liam and Olivia to my quarters of the house, so Olivia had her one small room to herself. It was a step up space-wise from the guest suite Liam had been staying in, but moving in the springtime would be ideal.

Later that afternoon, as I prepared to get dressed for a wedding, I sauntered up to Liam as he dressed for the occasion.

"Eva..." he drawled, watching my reflection in the mirror as I came up behind him. I ran my hand over his chest, then circled him until I could fall into his hug. His lips found my neck as he spun me to face him in the mirror. In nothing but my bra and thong, I'd hoped to entice him to a quickie, but it seemed now wasn't the time for it.

He nuzzled up along my neck but didn't let his hands stray toward my breasts or pussy.

"We'll be late."

"Hmm." I smiled as he kissed away. "Are you coming as my plus-one? Or as Constella security?"

"Both." He caught my chin and tipped my face up toward his for a deeper kiss. "There's no way you'd be anyone else's date."

"Normally, Franco and I put each other as our plus-ones. Since I never wanted to bring dates to these things. Nor did he." The wedding was for an older capo higher up in another family. They weren't rivals or allies. Since they operated in another city, it was more of a general expectation that we'd show up to represent the family. All of us would be there, Dante with Nina, Romeo with Tessa, and now, me with Liam.

I couldn't wait. It was exciting, exhilarating even, to come out as a couple at Nina's baby shower. We'd shown all those closest to the Constella Family that we were a couple. Tonight, at this wedding, we could show the whole world. Many families would be there to see that I'd finally claimed a man as my own.

"Now you've got me," he whispered before another long, tender kiss.

I did have him. Liam and Olivia had come to mean so much to me over such a short time, and I was excited each and every day to see what else could come. We were building toward something solid and lasting.

Leaving Olivia at home, we headed out with the others. Liam's answer about being both my date and security was an accurate assessment. He was with me. And on guard. Although he wasn't "working" and many Constella soldiers were with us all for security, I knew that Liam wouldn't turn off his defensive personality. He was always on, always alert and watching, but I was pleased that he could loosen up enough to be with me at the reception.

"Would you believe it if I told you that I'm not a fan of big parties like this?" he asked as we danced.

"How come?" I nodded. "Ah. Too many people in one place to follow? Always watching out?"

"Well, that too." He shrugged and slid his hand over my back to hold me closer. "I've never been enough of an extrovert to want to hang out like this. Too much small talk. Too many people to meet and remember."

"I think you're doing just fine." He was. I wouldn't have known that this wasn't his idea of fun. All night long, he'd been with me and the rest of my family that we'd come with. If he wasn't dancing with me or eating, we were together in a group. He chatted with Franco, Romeo, and Dante like he'd known them his whole life. Just the same, he smoothly slipped onto the dance floor with me to hold me and show me off.

I'd dressed to impress, and with the rate of him checking me out in this short gown, I'd captured his eye. It seemed like a constant struggle to keep our hands to ourselves.

"I'm doing fine because I'm with you," he replied after a gentle kiss to my cheek. "I fit in because I'm with you."

"Don't sell yourself short," I teased.

"But it's true. You're drop-dead gorgeous. Absolutely stunning in this dress." He playfully tugged at a curl that framed my face. "You're perfect. The perfect Mafia princess at the big ball."

I rolled my eyes at his silliness.

"But everyone who's watching us has to be wondering why the beautiful princess is with someone like me. I'm no one royal."

"You are to me." I kissed him to put an action behind the claim.

"You have to admit we're opposites. I've come from nothing and you're…"

"A spoiled, bratty slut?" I teased, reminding him of when we were last at an event like this one.

His responding grin was slow and sexy. "Wanna go find a closet?"

"Behave," I teased. *That* would really get attention. Too much attention. I didn't want to steal the night from the bride and groom, even if this was his third marriage and her second.

"Liam." Franco approached. He nodded at me too.

"Oh, want to cut in?" he asked, stepping back to let Franco take over.

He didn't. He held his hand up to show that he wasn't coming close to dance with me. The serious expression on his face didn't match one I'd expect on someone having a good time.

"What's wrong?" I asked in unison with Liam. We were that in sync, so quick to read Franco in the same moment.

"Rumors are running rife that Stefan is going to try to cause some trouble tonight."

I frowned, shaking my head. "But he's not here."

"He's still being a coward and hiding," Liam said. Only the Devil's Brothers showed themselves. Not here. No bikers would ever be here. Someone like Stefan Giovanni would've otherwise made it on to the guestlist for this wedding and reception, but the bastard was lying low after he tried to kidnap Nina and Tessa."

"True, but *she* was spotted ten minutes ago at the entrance." Franco turned and pointed out that woman. The tall redhead who'd shown up at the mansion and tried to claim she was Olivia's aunt.

"Fuck," Liam whispered, scowling immediately.

I narrowed my eyes. "You suspect she's working for the Giovannis?" I asked Franco.

"We figured she had to be working for Stefan or Reaper," Franco replied. "But one of the guards overheard her near the entrance just a minute ago. She's reporting to Stefan."

Liam shook his head. "What does this mean, then? She showed up trying to take Olivia…"

"Because she knows I value her," I said. "They know she's been living in the house. That's all Stefan needs to know—that she matters and is important to us."

Franco agreed, nodding and tracking the redhead through the crowd. Two Constella men followed her from a distance, not letting her out of their sight.

"Which means they'll see that she's not with us tonight," Liam said. "Here."

"No one brought children," Franco pointed out. "But I don't like this. Seeing that woman. If she's an indirect connection to Stefan, she can't be here simply to party."

I couldn't swallow down this uneasiness. It spread through me, almost like panic descending over me and taking control of my mind.

"I don't like this," I told Liam.

He held my hand, nodding. "The house is guarded," he reminded me unnecessarily.

"It is," Franco said. "But maybe if you're done with this party scene, it would give us all a better peace of mind if some of us headed home to watch over her."

We all stood by the Constella forces. But Olivia was just a baby, a precious innocent.

"I'm calling Danicia," I said, pulling out my phone from my clutch.

Liam nodded, and both men stood with me and waited for the doctor to pick up. She'd volunteered to babysit tonight. She was capable. So were the many guards at the house. But this was still a vulnerable setup—us being here and her at home.

"She's not answering." Liam grimaced at Franco.

He swore. "Fuck. We can't take chances. It could be nothing but—"

"Let's go." Liam was still holding my hand, and I was grateful for his grip. We didn't delay, rushing through the throngs of people in the crowd, urgently hurrying home.

Franco ran with us, weaving through the guests. "I'll call out a crew to head to the house as backup."

Even if it wasn't a worry, even if Danicia didn't answer her phone for a simple, valid reason, we would never slack in protecting Olivia.

The house was a fortress. I knew that. In the logical part of my mind, I wanted to stay convinced that Olivia was locked behind doors and the perimeter gate, safe with all the soldiers patrolling the property.

But anything was possible. Half of my iciness and putting up walls was a defense mechanism, but it was also the chronic buffering to bad things. To violence. To threats.

She will be okay. She will be fine. We're just overreacting. Things aren't adding up, but that doesn't mean she has to be hurt.

I winced, swallowing hard at the worrisome idea that we could've left her to be taken by our enemies.

I'd never forgive myself if anything happened to her. Never.

And by the tense grip of Liam's fingers wrapped around mine as we reached the exit, I knew he would never forgive himself either.

25

LIAM

"She'll be okay," Eva repeated frantically on the drive home. "She *has* to be okay."

I squeezed her hand, taking the risk to hold it as I drove as fast as I could. "She has to be," I agreed. Eva had more experience with this. She was more familiar with the layers of protection at that house. I'd been trained—so far—with more duties suited for spies and handling men we captured to interrogate.

Eva had grown up with this lifestyle, but when she repeated that panicked claim that Olivia would be all right, it sounded more like a desperate wish than a convinced belief.

It seemed that silence was a better option. As we rushed to the house, neither of us could confirm whether Olivia was all right or not. Eva kept calling Danicia to no avail. Franco had to be calling the guards at the house. No one was answering, and that couldn't be "okay".

We settled for not speaking, though, because trying to think of something to say seemed too difficult, a distraction we couldn't afford as we hurried to the house to check on Olivia.

Tense and stiff, we sat on the edge of our seats until I slammed to a stop in the long circular driveway to the mansion I'd more or less called home for months now.

I had my gun in my hand as I opened the door. Franco and other soldiers came to a stop abruptly, but I didn't waste time telling Eva to stay back. She wouldn't, so concerned and panicked to know that Olivia was safe. And I wanted her with me, anyway. She wasn't a liability, but a partner. If I needed backup with my daughter, she was who I wanted at my side, always.

The soldiers ran in with me, fanning out but also surrounding Eva. Franco rushed in hot on our heels. As we ran up the steps, two soldiers stayed back to check on the guards down on the ground. I ran past them so quickly that it was a blur. I didn't slow, dead set on finding Olivia, but from a quick glance, it seemed that no blood was spilled. The men were unconscious, but others could help them.

My goal was my daughter. My mission was to find out what the hell was going on and reset the balance of right and wrong. No one would touch my child for any reason without my say-so, and it was with a violent fury that I ran inside.

Olivia's cries reached me instantly. She lay on the floor within the pack and play structure, clutching Danicia's shirt over the edge of the short fencing. The doctor—babysitter for the night—was on the carpet, prone and unmoving.

"Olivia!" Eva cried out and hurried close with another guard.

I wouldn't have hesitated to rush to my crying baby for many reasons. Spotting the man running out toward the back of the house was one of the reasons I'd let Eva handle her instead.

She could comfort her. She had a good rapport with Olivia even though I was her father.

And while I counted on my woman, on my partner, I sprinted after the motherfucker who'd dared to sneak into the house.

"Liam!"

I turned slightly at Romeo's voice. He'd arrived, also alerted about all of this.

"This way!" He was running with me, helping me chase down the man who'd busted through a window in the back. Soldiers and guards swarmed the place. Other patrollers lay on the ground, all of them unconscious.

If this asshole brought backup, the arrival of the Constella forces would keep Eva and Olivia safe. They would. I was one of these men now, and I trusted them with my life, with the lives of my daughter and my future bride.

In the meantime, there was no fucking way on earth that I'd let someone else chase down this perp and kill them. This was my duty. This responsibility would fall on my shoulders, and it was with this rabid need to slaughter this trespasser that I ran harder and faster through the house with Romeo's shortcuts.

We burst into the back yard and cleared the patio, hot on the trail of this Devil's Brothers bastard. Spotlights popped on, set off with the motion sensors, and under the rays of illumination, the dark leather cut was visible. The biker's patch swished back and forth as he pumped his arms to run faster and evade us, but between me and Romeo, there wasn't a chance in hell that we'd let him escape.

Reaching the perimeter wall, we slowed to a stop and watched the biker drop down. A volley of gunfire rained down on us, and Romeo and I both dropped and rolled toward trees for safety.

Romeo gritted his teeth, shot in the arm. I covered for him, my new brother in arms, and I struggled against the parallels and flashbacks that hit me at the similarities of this situation and what I experienced overseas.

Shielding a comrade from gunfire. Lying on my stomach with a firearm, gauging where to fire and when. Checking that the soldier who was down would make it.

All the while, as the memories battered me, I focused on Romeo.

"That motherfucking MC will regret the day they ever tried to fuck with us," he growled as he compressed the bleeding injury.

I shushed him. While I didn't want to request that he shut up, the shooting was stopped. That silence was telling and with it, I took a chance to figure out where the bikers were shooting from and how many were out there. This double-trunked tree offered some protection, but it wasn't infallible.

Romeo clenched his teeth, not needing to be told twice.

I narrowed my eyes, straining to see and hear. I wished I had my rifle. I wanted some sights. Night-vision goggles would be best, and I suspected that was what these bikers were using.

What they hadn't taken into consideration was that I had other senses to rely on, other ways that I'd been trained to root out the enemy in dangerous territory.

Every one of those dumbasses stank. Of booze and weed, but mostly cigarettes. Staying as still as I could, I waited to acclimate to the darkness and mark them.

These weren't trained soldiers, men with advanced practice in covert ops like I was. And their clumsiness showed.

One fidgeted in the tree, showing me the shiny barrel of his gun. Another sniffed, likely fighting the urge to cough. Someone was closer yet, reeking of the cigarette he still smoked.

Stupid motherfuckers.

Romeo was pissed. I would be too if I were shot on my own property. He'd want to kill them all right now and then and end this war, but I had to agree with what Eva mentioned a long time ago. What Dante seemed to believe.

The Giovanni Family and Devil's Brothers MC had teamed up to attack the Constellas, but it might pay off to let them cancel each other out. The Giovannis hired a sniper previously, and that spoke of higher intelligence and a better skillset. But they had no money. The MC seemed to be raking in cash, but they were stupid motherfuckers.

If this was how these bikers fought—with gutsy, rash ambushes or sloppy, inexperienced attacks in the dark, I had to agree that these opponents deserved each other. Neither could beat the Constellas, regardless of their numbers.

I caught Romeo's attention and tried to wordlessly convey that he should stay still. The biker we'd chased was still on the ground, and he was the outlier I couldn't account for. But the other idiots in the trees who'd been waiting for him to come back?

They were sitting ducks. Dead men waiting.

This was far from the first guerilla form of combat I'd had to endure, and I doubted it'd be my last. I wasn't in the army anymore, but some things never fucking changed.

Romeo seemed to understand that I was moving out. Other Constella soldiers would come soon. They were busy at the house, but more would follow where we'd run.

Once they arrived, they'd prompt these bikers to fire their assault weapons again, recklessly, even blindly in a fit of trigger rage.

I couldn't let that happen. I refused to allow the asshole who made my daughter cry get away, either.

I drew in a steady breath to brace myself, and with a razor-edge of anticipation coursing through my blood and priming me to act, I eased out of the shadows of the trees and aimed for the first target I'd marked.

This is what happens when you scare my daughter.

I aimed and fired at the first man in the trees. He didn't scream, dead upon the bullet's impact between his eyes. Before another man could hit me, I dropped and rolled behind another tree.

Then I stepped out again, aiming at the second man.

This is what happens when you frighten my woman.

The second one was another successful pop of a bullet, through his open mouth. He fell, and another biker shouted, afraid as he fired his assault weapon into the next tree that I hid behind. I tensed, waiting out his gunfire.

Once all seemed to settle, once we were engaged in a terse game of suspense, I feigned a step to the left before whipping around to fire at the last biker hiding in the trees.

He was down, dead with two shots into his head, but I feared I'd receive the same as the biker we'd chased out here stood up and aimed his gun straight at my face.

Fuck.

26

EVA

"Oh, Liv." I hugged her close as she sobbed and cried. Her bright blue eyes were red-rimmed with how hard she'd cried. Her whole body was tense with fear, and as I clutched her tight, pressing my cheek to the top of her head, she clung to me. Her fingers cinched my dress and hair, but I didn't care if she yanked it out in her fists.

She could lean on me. She could rely on me to comfort her. I wasn't sure that I'd ever be able to let her go. Hearing her distressed cries broke my heart. In the same stroke, it infuriated me. If Liam caught that man and failed to kill him, I would. It would be my immense pleasure to pay back that asshole for scaring Olivia.

Worried that she could be injured, I leaned her back so I could look her over.

"Oh, my God." Nina rushed in, her face tight with worry. "Is she okay? Are you all right?"

Dante strode through, speaking with capos. Tessa ran in with them as well. I'd already caught sight of Romeo rushing with Liam for the man who was sneaking out the back. Franco was still checking on the fallen soldiers. And Danicia.

"Fucking dart gun," he reported as he crouched over the doctor who was more like a friend of the family.

I exhaled in relief that she wasn't wounded. Or worse, dead. We'd rushed in past the patrol guards lying on the floor too, and I wanted to assume they'd met the same fate—unconscious from a sedative, not killed.

Nina hugged us both, and as I lowered to sit, I ran my fingers over Olivia's face and neck, checking her over. Other than the angry flush of her crying so hard, she was unharmed. Untouched. No fingermarks, no red welts. No swelling areas of skin. She didn't react when I pressed on her skin, and I prayed that she would react or flinch if she'd been hurt. Miraculously, though, she was only scared, not bodily wounded.

"Was she hit?" Tessa asked as she came to my other side, hugging me and Olivia. All four of us cuddled on the couch, frantic to soothe Olivia.

"I can't see." A dart gun would've pierced her skin. That tiny of a hole would be hard to spot, but I felt and saw nothing.

"She would be out if she was hit with the dart," Nina assessed.

My breath shuddered out of me at the thought, and I held her close again, losing my control on a couple of tears. They streaked over my cheeks, and I sniffled as I hugged the crying baby close.

"She wouldn't be out. She'd be dead." A dart gun was dosed for an adult, not a baby.

"They'll review the footage of what they have," I said, more to myself than to them. Saying it out loud was a reassurance I needed, but both women nodded.

I rocked and hugged Olivia, rubbing her back as her cries lightened up. Nina kept her hand on my thigh, offering comfort. And Tessa stroked her hand up and down my back.

We caught our breath and stayed out of the way as the soldiers went through the house. Some were helping Danicia and the guards to stabilize. Others were scoping the place out for evidence of bugs or any explosives. More yet were following Franco and Dante's orders to secure the property.

It was a chaotic house full of commotion, but I clung to what they said about Liam.

"He and Romeo," Franco reported to Dante, who watched Nina carefully. "Both of them ran out after him."

My uncle's eyes narrowed. "Giovanni?" he guessed.

"No, someone near the back of the property said it's someone from the MC," a soldier replied. He had his phone to his ear, no doubt in touch with other men who ran out the back after Liam and Romeo.

"Those motherfucking bikers." Uncle Dante swore some more, pacing with Franco.

I breathed out long and hard, wishing all the tension could seep out of me with it. Liam wasn't alone. This wasn't like the other times he'd faced off with a member of the Devil's Brothers. In his short time of being with the family, he'd dealt with them often enough.

This wouldn't be a fight of one man against many. Romeo was with him, and I knew he'd look out for Liam like he would for a brother. Guards had rushed out there too. This entire property would be crawling with Constella men and no one would escape.

Liam will be all right. It was the same mantra that I'd told myself on the way here, worried beyond measure about Olivia when Danicia and the guards didn't answer.

He had to be okay because I needed him to live, to be here for the future we were destined to share. With Olivia. With any other child we could have.

While I clung to the hope that he'd be uninjured going after the man who'd broken in here, I also reminded myself that he wasn't just an ordinary soldier. He was a serviceman, a military employee who had ample experience to handle anything that came his way.

As the moments passed, my body remained tense. Only Olivia's calmer breaths soothed me. She grounded me as much as I bet I comforted her.

"I hate this constant of violence for her." I stroked my hand over her small body, reassuring her that I would protect her and reminding myself that she was here and well.

"Aren't you used to it?" Tessa asked. "You grew up in a life of violence."

I shrugged. "True. But I hate it for her." I sighed because there was no other alternative. Once you were in the Mafia life, there was no leaving it. It wasn't like a club that you could decline a renewal of membership to. "If I were to bring a baby into this world, I'd want him or her to live in more peace than this."

Nina huffed a dry laugh. "Tell me about it."

I frowned, glancing at her swollen belly. With Olivia asleep on my chest now, I could free one hand to pat her thigh in commiseration.

"You wouldn't want to start a family with Liam?" Tessa asked as everyone continued to bustle around us.

"We already have." When they both widened their eyes and dropped their mouths open at my reply, I shook my head. "Whoa. No, no, no." I pointed at Olivia. "I mean with her. With the three of us."

Tessa smiled and nodded. "You do look adorable, like a little ready-made family."

"But he's serious about staying with you, right?" Nina asked.

"We have yet to figure out where we'll live, but yeah."

"No… proposal?" Tessa asked.

I shrugged, careful not to wake Olivia. "Well, a girl can hope."

"He *seems* serious about you," Nina said.

"Then maybe he's just taking his time," Tessa guessed. "You guys hit it off quickly. Nothing wrong with pacing it out."

"And I'll be here for him," I vowed. I was certain, regardless of whether he proposed or we stayed dating like this, a mini family with Olivia, he would be my man. My only man. The only one I wanted for a serious commitment.

Even though it was whirlwind at first, we were settling into such a comfortable and relaxed companionship. He didn't get away with trying to control me, and I enjoyed him putting me in my place when I needed to tone down my attitude. Together, we made sense as unofficial co-parents for Olivia.

Nothing could go wrong between us. And that thought put a firm smile on my lips.

Here, at this moment as I soothed and cuddled Olivia after her scare, I knew deep down from the bottom of my heart that the father-and-daughter duo had stolen it. Liam had my heart. So did the sleeping baby on my chest.

I *loved* him. I loved her as well. With the clarity of that realization, my sense of urgency doubled. Liam had to be safe out there, avenging his daughter for how she was scared and targeted. But when he was done...

Come back to me. Come back to us.

Because I couldn't wait another minute to tell him that I loved him.

That once and for all, this Mafia princess had well and truly found her prince.

27

LIAM

A blast filled the air, but it wasn't my gun that fired. Nor was it the burly biker's.

Romeo grunted behind me, having rolled up onto his knees to shoot at the man who was about to blow my head off. "I knew you were a good shot, but..." he started as the biker groaned in agony.

The Devil's Brother gripped his hand—or what was left of it. The bloody pulp leaked everywhere, and the gun that dropped was too slippery to fetch. "You motherfucking asshole!" Romeo got him right in the hand, disarming him.

I raised my brows and fired at the biker. Twice. His shattered kneecaps were beyond saving now. Screaming instead of cursing at us, he fell to the ground.

"But *damn*, are you a good shot."

I nodded. "Thanks for the backup," I quipped dryly. I wasn't here for praise about my marksmanship. I earned the compliment from years of service, but right now, I wanted to get some goddamn answers from this fucker before we killed him.

"What were you sent here to do?" I let Romeo aim his gun at the man. Not his face, but at his cock. It seemed that the prince of the

Constella Family wanted his victims to die emasculated. I kept my gun trained at the asshole's face.

"Fuck you."

Romeo pulled the trigger.

The man cried out loudly. And rolled onto his back. He covered what remained of his dick with his bloody hand.

"What were you sent here for?" I demanded.

"I was gonna take the baby hostage. Reaper wants her for leverage."

My blood boiled hotter. I clenched my teeth so hard that my jaw ached like it never had before, but I refused to pull the trigger.

"Then what?" Romeo asked.

"Then I was gonna burn the goddamn house down. Reaper's still mad about you motherfuckers having so much power." He spat at us, still so vindictive even at our mercy.

I thought back through all that the mighty Constella family had done already. Dante took Nina and refused to let her honor that bet. Then Romeo killed the MC's smarmy lawyer. I supposed they could claim a right to be mad, but I didn't give a shit. They were bad people. When bad people did bad things, they only deserved it in kind.

"What about Giovanni?" Romeo demanded.

"He's angrier than Reaper. Sounds like Dante and Stefan go way back, and he's pissed that old friendships don't last."

"Tough shit," Romeo replied. "Stefan isn't half the man he used to be, when he was worthy of our friendship and alliance."

The idiot laughed, as though he could actually experience anything other than pain until we finished him off. "We don't need you fuckers now. No one does. That's why we're gonna end you all."

"I doubt that."

"No. If they combine, it'll be too many to face at once," Romeo said. "If they teamed up in attacking us, we would be outnumbered." He looked at me with a grave scowl. "No matter how damn good of a shot you are, we would be outnumbered."

"And we got an alliance that'll keep us safe. From you. From the law." He snickered. "We're fucking immune like you'd only dream of."

Immune? From being caught? "Congratulations on bribing a cop," I drawled sarcastically.

"Like that's never been done before," Romeo replied.

"Not a cop. Reaper's got us a middle man, a connection between the Devil's Brothers and the governor's office. He can put more heat on y'all."

"Who is it?" I asked.

"Like hell am I giving you a name. Fuck you to hell. I'm gonna laugh in your faces when you can't beat 'em."

Romeo and I shared a look.

"All you're going to do now is serve as another reminder for Reaper to think twice." I pulled the trigger, killing him with one shot between his eyes.

I loosened my shoulders, but I was still too tense to come close to relaxing. I was glad and relieved that this man was dead. But the news he'd shared with us wasn't heart-warming.

"What middle man?" I asked Romeo.

He shook his head, not pleased about this development. "I don't know, but I don't like the sound of this."

"Dante and Franco haven't heard about it?" I knew I was sometimes pushing the boundaries of my position. I wasn't a capo. I was a new recruit. But the men confided in me in such a way that made me feel like I was "in" with them.

"No." He rubbed his face and winced when he moved his arm too much. "But it's nothing new. Bribed officials and all. My father doesn't rely on it much anymore. Easier to deal with the commercial sector of funders."

With the number of lobbyists out there, I wasn't surprised. In or out of the government, corruption was everywhere, braided into the fabric of the economy.

"We need to secure the properties better. If they're going to continue to come at us, this can't be happening. No one can be sneaking in."

I nodded. "Are you suggesting a lockdown?"

"Damn near it. We have to. If they're banking on immunity and protection from the law with this middle man in the governor's office, they'll only get cockier and attack more." Romeo looked up as more men rushed in. He gave them directions where the men were, but he dismissed them from offering to assist him.

"Just a graze," he said of his wound.

I waved them off.

Before we walked back to the house, I glanced at the men I killed.

"We've faced worse," Romeo said. "We can handle this."

"Hell, I have too." I'd faced many hardships and horrors over the years I served.

I checked that he wasn't dizzy from blood loss as we walked.

"But that was in war, in the army. For the military."

Now, though, the stakes were higher. Much higher. I was far more vested in this version of "war" even though the adversaries were Mafia men and motorcycle gangsters.

It wasn't the time to get comfortable. With this dead biker's news of a different layer of support they were leaning on, we had to buckle in for more danger.

And I'd face it head on. I would do anything to protect these people, but most of all, Eva and Olivia.

I was vested in *them*. In us. In the future we would have one day, but not while we had to fear more attacks.

As we walked back to the house, I saw the irony in the timing of this all. Right when I wanted to tell Eva that I wanted her to be my wife, to propose, I'd need to save that conversation for when it made more sense.

I went all my life not realizing I wanted a traditional family, not that the Constellas were a conventional family unit. A kid and a wife. But now that I'd had a taste of it, I would make it happen, one way or another.

I came here not knowing what direction my life would take me, but I knew now. And I'd never lose sight of where I belonged.

28

EVA

Liam returned after I'd already fallen asleep. Tessa received a call from Romeo that they were safe and the perpetrator was killed. *All* the perpetrators were killed near the back property wall.

Just like I'd known he would, Liam handled the danger well. He was my soldier man, undefeatable, but I still sighed with relief at the news.

"He's still out there with them," Tessa reported to me. "Still cleaning up and discussing with them what to do next."

I yawned, nodding at her as I held Olivia to me. After the excitement of getting ready for the wedding—that felt like it happened a week ago, not hours ago—and the worry about not reaching the house, I was exhausted. "I expect he'll be busy yet."

"Heading to bed?" Nina asked.

"Yes." I didn't want to sound flippant or dismissive. I'd been tense waiting for word from Liam, but this was the second episode of that specific anxiety. When he went to plant those bugs at the MC's compound, I was up so late, worried to the nth degree. Then tonight, anxious for word after he ran out of the house after that man, I experienced more of that gut-wrenching nervousness.

I wasn't blowing anything off. I was desperate to see him. To kiss him. To check him over with my own eyes and hands and *know* he was all right.

But I also had faith in him. If he was wounded or needing any kind of help, Romeo wouldn't lie about it.

Besides, this break-in would necessitate a lot of strategy and follow-up. Uncle Dante didn't only raise me to be guarded. He'd also trained me from early on that sometimes, the men had meetings that took precedence over all else.

I could be patient. With Olivia comforting me, we could rest until he was prepared to call it a night. He would never suffer nagging pressure from me to check in. I got it. I really did.

Olivia didn't stir as I took her to bed. I didn't like letting her sleep in our bed with us, but since it was just me right now, I wanted to have her close. I laid her in bed and formed a line of pillows so she couldn't roll out. She didn't move much in her sleep. She was a cuddler, but not a busy toddler kicking and moving all over in her sleep. Liam and I were like that, too, so the risks of co-sleeping were likely lower, but tonight was an exception.

I wanted to be there for her if she woke, and I wanted her close if I did. After facing the fear—even slight—of losing her, I would be clingy. And I wouldn't apologize for it.

"I love you, lil Liv." I kissed her forehead after I laid her down. Then I shed my dress and slipped on some pajamas before I cleaned off my makeup.

Snuggling in with her was heaven, and I couldn't help myself. I kissed her head again and fought the tears of relief that she was okay. That she was safe.

Olivia mattered so much to me, and I knew that I had to tell Liam. It felt wrong to know that I loved him and his daughter and not share that revelation.

Late in the night, he trudged into our room and showered. I was so sleepy that I didn't get up, but I felt the weight of his stare before he went into the bathroom.

Without a word but yawning heavily, he climbed into bed and

spooned me. Keeping his arm over me, his hand over mine on Olivia's belly, I was sandwiched between the two people who'd come to mean the whole world to me.

And when I slept, it was a blissful darkness of no nightmares.

Olivia woke us in the morning, and I would never in my life forget how.

"Mama. Mama, Mama, *Mama!*"

I blinked at the new name and smiled instantly.

Until she paired the wakeup call with a smack to my face. It was likely intended to be a pat, but she hadn't mastered the fine art of measuring her strength.

"Mama?" I asked her, wincing as I rubbed the eye she'd smacked.

She clapped, proud that she'd gotten me to reply. "Mama wake. Mama wake."

Oh, my heart. I sniffled, on the verge of happy tears.

"Mama's awake, huh?" Liam asked her.

His voice was husky with sleep, and I smiled wider at the sound of him like this. I loved how drowsy and relaxed he was. His bedroom eyes were potent, but his sleepy voice never failed to jumpstart my libido.

"I guess so," I told him. As I rolled over to face him, I smacked into his hand.

"Ow," I said, rearing back to rub my other eye. He must have been up for a while, despite that sleepy, sexy voice. As I slumped onto my back, Olivia dropped onto me and hugged me at an awkward angle. Her diaper rested on my forearm, trapping me, and I blinked at two realizations at once.

Her diaper wasn't soggy. Liam had already gotten up and changed her.

That wasn't all he'd done, rising before me.

He'd procured a ring box. It was open, showing me a sparkling diamond ring. That was what I'd rolled over to smack into.

"What do you say, *Mama?*"

I blinked slowly, wondering if I was still dreaming.

It was a gift of the highest manner for Olivia to take it upon herself to call me mama. No one ever used that word around her except when reading books. Maybe some pre-k cartoon shows, like the one with the annoying voice for the cow character.

She'd put it together to call me mama, and I was honored that she saw me as a mother in her young life.

But a ring? Liam had been hinting at getting serious with me, and we were loosely planning to move in the spring.

I told Tessa and Nina that I wanted to commit, but he was proving how much he intended to connect himself with me.

"Wait a minute." I scooted up on the bed to sit facing him. "Was that a proposal?"

He sighed, wincing a little bit that endeared him to me all the more. "Well, it wasn't my original proposal."

You sweet, sexy man. "Yeah? How'd that one go?" I smiled, eyeing him with so much love that I swore I'd burst.

"I brought it to the wedding last night. I thought I could get you somewhere quiet near the end of the night. Maybe I could sneak you off into… another closet."

I rolled my eyes but smiled, loving that this could be our little joke.

"But then…" He raised his brows. "We didn't exactly stay until the end."

I nodded, sobering at that reminder.

"So this morning, I thought I could have Olivia hand the box to you."

I held her close and kissed her cheek. "No go?"

He shook his head. "A blow out. I never changed a diaper so fast. I was worried the stink would wake you and we'd lose the element of surprise."

"Uh-oh," I teased her.

"Uh-oh!" She loved exclaiming it loudly.

"Then she lost interest in holding the box to hand it to you." He frowned at the wet corner. "Then she wanted to gnaw on it." He wiped the corner off on the sheet. "And then she decided to give you a new name and wake you up. And here we are."

He held the box closer, smiling at me with so much love in his gaze.

"I love you, Eva. Will you make me the happiest man alive and be my wife? The mother of my children?"

I leaned in to kiss him, brushing against the ring box he held out. "Yes, Liam. I would love to be your wife."

"Mama!" Olivia wedged in, hugging me close.

"And I would love to be the mother of your children."

He kissed me harder, keeping me close. When we parted, he took the ring out of the box and slid it onto my finger. "Perfect fit."

I smiled, staring at it fondly. "It is. Just like you are a perfect fit in my life." I kissed Olivia's cheek. "Both of you. I love you, Liam."

"I love you too." After another heated kiss, he got a smug smile on his lips as he gazed at my hand and the glittering diamond on my finger. "I had Tessa and Nina help pick the ring when you had Olivia at a swim lesson."

I gasped. "They knew all along?"

"Romeo too. He came to give me advice as well. He teased me the whole time that he knew from the moment he introduced us that we'd hit it off."

I rolled my eyes. "Oh, that's silly. He did not."

"Hmmm. I think I might have." He pulled me closer until we snuggled with Olivia climbing over us both.

"You knew the moment you saw me that you'd want to marry me?"

"Well, I knew I wanted *something* with you. And I'm glad we both fought hard enough to find what we have."

"And what's that, my handsome fiancé?"

"A very bright future."

We kissed to seal it.

While the morning started on a good note—a proposal and being dubbed Mama—we walked into the kitchen to face much more serious and bad news.

Over breakfast, everyone congratulated us. Danicia was there as well, recovered from being drugged already. It really did seem that everyone knew about Liam's plans to make it official with me. Franco had helped quite a bit in securing the paperwork to have me officially adopt Olivia, too. Once we married, she would really be my daughter, and he would be my husband.

I couldn't wait. I'd been eager for a purpose and for something to concentrate on, and I sure had gotten my wish granted in that regard. And I'd never take a second of it for granted. As everyone talked about how good of a match we were, I realized how much I'd changed—and how I hadn't, staying true to myself—after meeting Liam. No longer just an icy Mafia princess, I was someone who'd be married to a wonderful man. I was already recognized as a mother. Both roles, being Liam's wife and Olivia's mother, felt like a dream come true, a dream I hadn't even known I'd been waiting for until I met them.

After the celebratory moments, Uncle Dante filled us in on what happened last night. We had most of the details now, according to the surveillance cameras and what the guards and Danicia remembered. Everyone was recovering from the darts, and that was the best news we could've hoped for.

Liam and Romeo also shared what happened when they chased the biker to the property wall. I knew they were watering it down. Their summaries were brief and to the point, but conclusive so we wouldn't have any questions and would feel satisfied with answers. I would never ask Liam how many people he killed. I didn't want to know, and I didn't want him to think that his kill count mattered to me. Part of his appeal was his rugged masculinity, and even if it did reduce my feminism, knowing he could go to the extreme of killing people made him all the more attractive. He was no coward. He was a bold fighter, fighting the good fight with us.

"A middle man?" Nina asked after Liam and Romeo finished talking. "Who could be this middle man in the governor's office?"

"Oscar Morelli," Franco said as he entered the spacious kitchen, overhearing us as he came into the room. "I had Andy and a couple other spies look into it based on who the bikers were talking to."

Romeo narrowed his eyes and nodded. "That sounds familiar."

Franco seemed pleased with this information. "I'm not surprised. Once we tracked where Reaper's bike was going, we realized he was making a habit of visiting someone near the governor's house. Once we had a name, we looked up surveillance, and it added up."

"He's definitely the one helping the MC?" Dante asked.

"Yes." Franco nodded. "We've got video of him meeting with Reaper. Then our hackers found a trail of transactions. It seems Oscar's got a fondness for coke and young whores, which Reaper provides."

"When do we go after him?" Romeo asked, glancing at his father. "If we kill him, they don't have an ace up their sleeve anymore."

"Always one step ahead," Dante agreed.

"Not so fast," Franco warned. "I have a feeling it won't be a *we* situation." He pointed at Liam. "More like a sniper and expert marksman situation."

Liam nodded as he rubbed his chin. "Why? Is he a hard man to get alone?"

"Very," Franco replied. "He's heavily guarded and seems super paranoid. It would be a challenge to get to him directly."

I squeezed his hand, nodding at him.

"Today? Or tonight?" Liam asked, seeming to understand that I was giving him permission. He didn't need permission from me, but we were hoping to ask someone to watch Olivia here while we had dinner, just the two of us in our room, to celebrate our engagement.

This would put a damper on our plans, but I understood. This was the way of the Mafia life.

"Yes. The sooner, the better," Franco said. "Before he can try to hide any better."

"You say jump, and I'll jump."

Franco smiled, just now spotting the ring on my finger. "Ah. Planning to celebrate tonight?"

I waved him off. "I can wait." I felt like I'd been waiting all my life for someone like Liam, a strong man who could understand me and be able to handle me. But one more night wasn't impossible. He'd proven this morning that he wanted to give me all of his days and every one of his nights.

"Shouldn't take long if we leave soon." Franco tipped his head toward the door. "We can talk about the details on the way."

"All right." Liam stood, but he didn't hurry to follow after Franco. First, he downed his coffee. Then he leaned in toward Olivia and kissed the top of her head. "Be good for your mama," he told her and backed away before she got him with a syrupy spoon.

"Who do I need to be good for?" I teased him as he approached me to kiss me goodbye.

"Me," he replied. After he framed my face, he kissed me so tenderly that I wanted to swoon. But he didn't let go. Slanting toward my ear, he whispered, "But I like it when you're bad for me too."

I smiled, pressing my lips together to keep from grinning.

Watching him leave was getting easier. He'd proven time and time again that he was capable of surviving all odds against any other man. Each time he headed out to do something for the family's security, I knew that he wouldn't be rash or foolish.

He couldn't, not when he had so much to live for and enjoy with me and Olivia. Even though he could be stoic and guarded—like me— at times, it was impossible for me to miss the happiness and zest for life that shone in his light-blue eyes. They pierced me, reaching to my soul every time we locked gazes, and in his loving stare, I felt the excitement he couldn't hide. The excitement to start the rest of his life with me at his side.

"I'll be back," he called out before he left through the doorway in the direction toward the garages, where Franco had gone.

Yes, you will. I agreed with his claim, and I knew he wasn't saying it to be cocky or sound smart.

I had all confidence that he'd come home to me. And when he did, we'd spend the night celebrating the next step of our relationship.

Maybe with some more of that "practice" to make a younger brother or sister for Liv...

I sighed, not caring if everyone noticed how dreamy I sounded.

"That was fast," Uncle Dante teased.

I shrugged. "Is there any set speed at which a woman can meet her fiancé?"

"No." He shook his head. "I'm just taking advantage of the moment to throw that judgment back at your face. You were so critical of me and Nina hitting it off when we did. You claimed it was too hurried."

"Sometimes, life determines it all." I pondered how it all happened so far. "Because if you hadn't met Nina and fallen in love, maybe Tessa never would have met Romeo and fallen in love. And if Tessa weren't in our home, I might not have ever met Liam and Olivia."

A wide smile stretched my lips.

Now, we just have to have some hope that Franco could move on from Chloe one day.

It was infectious, this falling-in-love business. And no one would ever hear me complaining about it.

29

LIAM

Heading to a golf course to kill an assistant to the governor didn't sound like a smart idea. I didn't hesitate to tell Franco that as he drove us there.

"I'm not saying we should wait," I argued as I sat in the passenger seat and cradled my gun between my knees. He'd taken one of the beat-up trucks for this assignment, all the better to hide and disguise ourselves should anyone be following us.

"The sooner we do this, the better," he reminded me.

I got that. I did. The Constella Family didn't do anything rash. I wasn't sure if it was tradition, self-control, or learning from mistakes in the past, but Dante ran a tight ship. He expected all of us, from Romeo, to Franco, and all the way down to every soldier, to do their best. Doing our best included planning things out.

And setting up an op at a wide-open golf course seemed like a plan that might need more consideration.

"We need to always stay one step ahead of the game," he added.

"I get that, I do." I splayed my hand at the window, indicating the open landscape. "But a golf course? It's a vulnerable area to attempt this."

Franco shook his head. "It'll be harder later. He's taking advantage of the mild weather today. I mean, it's seventy in late February."

I chuckled. "It does feel bizarre to have it this warm."

"Eh. It won't last. And listen, man, I'm not trying to rush this for the sake of hurrying. He'll be out of town a lot next month, and it'll be harder to reach him."

"Yeah. I can see that. But..." I shrugged, knowing my argument faded the closer we got to the point we'd studied on satellite images. The courses were too crowded, surprisingly, and I realized that this might go smoothly after all.

I was most used to being asked to perform as a sniper in remote locations, in warzones. Not golf courses for the elite members of politics.

"Never mind," I said, waving him off. "I'll get it done."

He chuckled. "You'll be back in no time. Congrats, by the way."

I smiled, relaxing with the thought of Eva on my mind again. "Nina already said she'd watch Olivia so Eva and I could celebrate over dinner."

"I thought you were planning on proposing at that wedding."

I smirked. "At the *end* of the wedding, but we didn't stay until the end."

"Ah. Right. And Olivia's not too shaken up?" he asked.

"No. She was scared last night, but she's all right today. That's why we wanted to keep her at home, with someone she's familiar with, like Nina."

"Makes sense."

I blew out a long breath as we neared where I'd set up my scope. We had to time it right down to the tee—literally, the tee time of that hole where Oscar Morelli would be setting up to swing at. "I hate that she'll always be on the cusp of danger," I admitted, feeling free to speak my mind with Franco, "but this is the life I want. With Eva. Working with you, Dante, and Romeo."

"She'll be safe. Anything can happen, but we have men in place. Last night prompted us to review our security measures, and you can trust that Dante is bothered about this. With Nina pregnant and at that house?" He huffed a laugh. "He won't take any chances. Not with her or their baby, not with any of us. It's a real family here, Liam. Not just a job."

"I can see that." But setting up the scope and taking my shot while Franco served as my lookout was just a job. Just another kill. Keeping myself dissociated from it helped me to not dwell on it. Maybe that was how my buddy Ethan in Brooklyn coped with his decision to consider hiring himself out as an elite hitman on call.

The world was full of danger. There were too many "bad guys", and I was coming to really see how the Constellas weren't all bad.

On the way back after the successful hit, Franco received a call.

"Please, no. Nothing can come up now." I laughed as he shot me a look.

I meant it, though. I wanted *one* day to share with Eva, to commemorate my admittedly poorly executed proposal.

Franco listened to whoever spoke on the other end, and I gritted my teeth at his tense expression.

Shit. Something's happened. Because of course something has.

"Where? Near Brooklyn?" he asked the caller.

Okay, nothing to do with anyone at the house, then. Sometimes, this guy amazed me. He was on top of so many other capos, all the soldiers, like a chief commander. How he kept track of so many operations and employees was beyond my imagination, and I bet I'd never fail to look up to the man who was already more like a friend than a boss.

"Does it look like the Giovannis did it?" he asked.

Those fuckers. I shook my head, looking out the window both to watch the scenery blur by and also to check the passenger mirror for anyone following us or noticing us. I would never lose that paranoid nature I couldn't shut off. It was simply a part of who I was. Always on edge. Always alert.

Especially after killing a prominent but crooked assistant to a politician.

"Huh. Yeah. Okay. Well, no. I'm headed back to Dante. You can fill him in. Yeah. Yeah. Bye."

Once he disconnected, I rolled my head on the cushion to face him. "Now what?" I kept my tone neutral, not whiny. They were paying me very well. I was marrying into the family. But I wasn't afraid to stand up for myself if it seemed like they would be taking advantage of me. I was likely the only decent sniper they had in the organization. I assumed that not with inflated confidence but with the years I'd put in to become the specialized firearms expert that the army wanted me to be.

"One of the businesses was attacked."

I exhaled a long breath.

"No, it's nothing you need to deal with."

Now I felt like an ass, slacking. "Hey, I'm here for whatever you need, but—"

"No. Not this. They fucking shot the place up. Only one employee survived, and I'll need someone to track them down to talk with them. Sounds like he or she is the only witness."

I nodded, absorbing this news. It really was one thing after the other. "I can ride along and help."

"To find a witness who's probably scared shitless after their workplace was shot up?" He grunted a bitter laugh. "Yeah, that will take a while. It sounds like they ran after the shooting happened."

"Can't say I'd blame them. What business was it?"

"A deli. Just a cover business. Sometimes, they packaged drugs in the basement."

"And you think the Giovannis are behind it?" I was getting sick of that rival family already. They were a thorn in my side, and I'd only just joined the Constella Family. Dante had to be exhausted from putting up with them—former friends or not.

"Tony, the capo who called me, seems to think it's something the Giovannis did with the way it happened. I'm not so sure, though. Another soldier seemed ready to swear it wasn't them."

I sighed. It already sounded like a hassle. "So, now what? Comb through surveillance and track what you can?"

"That and finding this surviving witness and seeing what they say. No." He shook his head. "Scratch that. What's next for *you* is bringing you back to the house so you can have your date night with Eva."

"Hey, security first."

He nodded, solemn but not gloomy. Like this was just another day in the life for him. "It is. Until this becomes a situation where I need your specific skills and talents, we have many other men on the force who can assist me."

"Okay. But if you ever need me… or just want my help."

He parked at the house, nodding and smiling a bit. "Then I'll call you." He held out his hand for a shake, and I shook it.

"You're a good man, Liam. I'm glad you're *really* staying in the family. Marrying into it and all."

I nodded, hesitating before getting out of the truck. Franco was married to his job. He was a hardcore man who managed so many things and dealt with so many people in the organization. I didn't want him to look at me as just someone else to move or place on assignments.

"Go on. Have a good night. You and Eva deserve a chance to celebrate." He tipped his head toward the door.

I sighed, hating that he was dismissing himself to the job. Sure, it was a priority to be on, but the man needed to take care of himself too. Going nonstop and working without any balance would burn him out.

I'll be keeping an eye on you, buddy. He was a friend more than anything else, and I would never slack in taking care of those close to me.

Now wasn't the time to argue with him, though. He was determined to stay working, not slow down or delegate the supervision of this issue to the other capo, Tony, or any other soldier.

Defeated in this argument, I reminded him once more to call me if he needed or wanted help, then I headed up the steps to go find my girls.

It was surreal how different one day could make. Last night, Eva and I rushed up these stairs and hurried past the patrolling guards who'd been shot with the tranq darts. Today, the pair of soldiers standing on guard smiled at me and nodded as I reached the entrance.

"How'd it go, Liam?" one asked.

"Perfectly."

I entered and went upstairs to find Eva. We had hours before our attempt at a dinner date could start, but that wouldn't keep me from her. She, too, needed to keep a balance in life.

Olivia had grown so quickly, already nearing her second birthday, and it was crazy how fast life blurred by. She'd reached so many milestones and she was so fast on her feet now, jumping, running, and leaping. Eva kept up with her, but it added up. Toddlers, quite frankly, were no joke. Every night, we fell asleep too soon because Liv wore us out during the day, and Eva handled her more when I was off on assignments.

Still, I wouldn't have it any other way. And I could tell she wouldn't either.

I found them napping in the bedroom. One of those annoying cartoon shows was on, but it was muted, thank God. Instead of waking them, I walked up to the edge of the bed and watched them resting together. Even though Olivia seemed normal and like her usual happy, peppy self earlier, there was a good chance the stress and trauma from last night could linger yet. For Eva, too. We were both so worked up when we worried that something could be happening at home. That sort of distress didn't just fade after the incident was finished.

A little bit of guilt lingered. Here I was, able to relax and have downtime, but Franco was out there, still working hard.

Maybe I should've just gone along with him. Even for a little bit to assess the scene. Capos didn't have partners as far as I could tell, but if he wanted a partner on the clock, I'd step up and fill that role if he wanted me to.

After all, they're just napping here. I wasn't in the mood to wake Eva or Olivia. They needed their rest, but since I was up, I could go join Franco on that case.

Or... I gave in to a wide but silent yawn, realizing I could take care of myself and go for what *I* wanted at the moment. I showered quickly not wanting to get the bed dirty from when I took my shot in the wood line at the edge of that golf course.

Then I climbed into the bed with Eva and Olivia.

The instant I wrapped my arm around Eva's side and placed my hand on Olivia's back, all was right in my world again.

I'll help Franco later. But right now, I'm exactly where I need to be.

I closed my eyes, breathing in the familiar scent of Eva's shampoo. Past that, I detected the clean baby scent that I hoped Olivia never outgrew.

We were safe, and we'd stay together, our own little family within the larger one.

My future was full of hope, and I'd never lose sight of that blessing, no matter what.

30

EVA

I wasn't sure Franco would make it for dinner, but I hoped he'd come for a little bit. Yesterday, Liam told me that Franco was called away for a shooting on the drive back after he assassinated the middle man the MC relied on. So, like usual, Franco was on the job.

Dante and Romeo were on edge, waiting for the MC's reaction to their "ace" being removed. Killing that assistant to the governor was just another way of staying ahead of our enemies, but I could tell Nina and Tessa wanted both of them to focus on family time for a change.

"Well, he's got to eat," Tessa said when I asked aloud if anyone heard from Franco and if he'd come.

"He can pick up something on the way," Dante said. "But I agree. He needs to take a break every now and then. He's been running nonstop ever since I met you," he said, smiling fondly at Nina.

Which meant Franco had been working overtime for almost a year. Deep down, I suspected the reason. It was precisely what we were talking about before Tessa and Romeo had their engagement party.

Franco was now the odd one out. When Dante met Nina, we were all reacting to how deeply and quickly they'd fallen for one another.

And that was my uncle, who never cared to even date over the course of a couple of decades, preferring to stay committed to working and running the Constella empire.

Then when Romeo and Tessa got together, it was inevitable to feel like love was in the air but not touching all of us. I'd suffered from that particular envy then too. I chatted about it with Franco.

But now, with me and Liam together... Franco was the only one who'd stayed solo. It wasn't by choice. He just couldn't seem to help himself get over Chloe from so long ago.

"Well, if he doesn't come to dinner," I said, "I'm taking food over to his house."

"Yeah, that's a good idea," Liam said. "And I'll help him with this latest attack."

"Good."

We all turned at Franco's entrance. Like he was prone to do, he walked right into the conversations, already overhearing a snippet of them.

"I welcome your help, Liam," Franco said as he took his seat at the table. He slumped down and sighed, rubbing his face.

If anyone's going to tell him he's working too hard... I've got my bets on Nina.

My fiancé beat her to it, and bluntly. "Franco. You're working too fucking hard."

I swatted his arm.

"Bad word, Dada," Olivia announced.

"Sorry, baby girl." He kissed her brow.

"This case is nothing like what I thought it'd be," Franco admitted.

"How come?" Dante asked as he handed over a plate of food Nina, Tessa, and I prepared. Last night, the chef outdid himself making a delicious meal for Liam and me to share in our wing of the mansion. It was a simple but classy date, and we both felt better knowing Olivia was in the house with Nina, close by in case we were needed after the trauma of the previous night.

"Tony's convinced it's the work of the Giovannis, but I'm not sure. The scene is..." He winced, glancing at Olivia. As though he was worrying about her listening. "It was grisly. Not like making a statement and just making a hit on us, but a massacre."

I cringed. "That's not what they're after. If they want to attack, they will, but not to the point of wasting ammo, right?" I glanced between Liam and Franco, then looked at Romeo.

"I agree. That would be more like the work of the Devil's Brothers," Romeo replied.

"Yeah, but get this. Edward was helping Tony in the area, and he suggested this could be someone else. Like Donny."

Dante furrowed his brow. "Donny Domino?"

Liam grunted a laugh. "Wait, that's actually his name? Donny Domino?"

Franco nodded. "*Was* his name. Donny was gunned down when the Devil's Brothers attacked the Domino Family and ended them."

"Maybe there were more survivors than anyone realized," Romeo said.

"But why attack a deli owned by the Constella organization?" Franco argued. He sat back and closed his eyes as he rubbed his face. The poor man looked so worn down that I felt like one of us should intervene. Liam already said he'd step up and assist, and I knew I could count on him. He, too, watched Franco with concern.

"And then the witness. The one employee who survived. They ran so far and fast, it's been hell tracking them down."

"Bad word, Franco."

We all smiled at Olivia.

Franco nodded. "Sorry, Livy."

"We'll head after this witness tomorrow, then," Liam said. "I can be a fresh set of eyes on what you're looking at."

To my surprise, Franco didn't protest. He really was at the end of his rope if he wouldn't automatically insist on being able to handle it himself.

"But tonight, we're all here together," Franco said. "Let's eat." He picked up his wine glass. "Drink." He did, taking a long swallow. "And be merry while we can be."

"Hey, we're all here." Liam winked at me. "We should just elope or something."

I mocked a gasp, feigning shock. "What? Elope? I'll need a grand production of a wedding. The celebration of the century, fit for a princess." I fluffed my hair back over my shoulder and posed with a dramatic, snooty face. I got what I was going for—Olivia's laugh at my goofiness.

He grabbed the back of my neck and pulled me close for a kiss. "So long as you're *my* princess, I'll give you whatever you want."

I arched a brow, smiling wide. "Anything?"

"Everything you want," he promised.

"Even a brother or sister for Olivia?" I bit my lip to keep from giggling. It was too much fun teasing this man. But this was no joke. I meant it, and I knew he was on the same page as me.

"Of course," he replied, kissing me once more. "We'll *practice* tonight."

I can't wait. For tonight, and every night for the rest of our lives.

We'd always be surrounded by danger, but I knew that my man, my future, would always do his best to come back to us.

Printed in Great Britain
by Amazon